PRAISE FOR *Whatever Makes You Happy*

"From Aristotle to Edith Wharton . . . from laughter therapy to bedroom farce, this novel is a dictionary of delights." —O: *The Oprah Magazine*

"Grunwald explores the meaning of happiness, drawing inspiration from poets and pop icons. . . . Readers may find themselves considering what underlies their own happiness—and what they would risk to find more."
—*People*

"Smart and exceedingly charming." —*W*

"Sally's quest for personal fulfillment allows Grunwald to muse on the roots of happiness, mining sources as diverse as Aristotle and Charles Schulz to present a provocative array of answers. *Whatever Makes You Happy* is a satisfying portrait of upper-middle-class angst. But it is also the tale of a woman's pursuit of a life philosophy—and through that search, readers may discover stepping stones for their own." —*More*

"Grunwald is smart, funny and talented." —*Publishers Weekly*

"Engaging." —*Kirkus Reviews*

"Grunwald's interweaving of scholarly quotations about happiness and excerpts of real-life research on the matter cleverly ground this novel, in which the main character is on the verge of spinning out of control as she searches for her own brand of happiness. Chock-full of penetrating and wry perceptions . . . recommended."
—*Library Journal*

"A solid book with a likeably complex, funny, truthful woman at its center . . . Grunwald writes smoothly. . . . Her Sally Farber lives and breathes on the page, thanks to the author's excellent touch for dialogue and for creating believable emotional moments." —*The Buffalo News*

"Believing that she's only 'researching' the pursuit of happiness, Sally Farber searches for that ephemeral quality in all sorts of droll places—from the writings of Voltaire to the Laughter Institute to the bed of a famous artist. This book comprises the best of both reads: a serious romp, and a saucy philosophical sashay." —JACQUELYN MITCHARD, author of
The Deep End of the Ocean and *The Breakdown Lane*

Also by Lisa Grunwald

FICTION

New Year's Eve
The Theory of Everything
Summer

NONFICTION

Women's Letters
Letters of the Century
(with Stephen J. Adler)

FOR CHILDREN

Now, Soon, Later

Whatever Makes You Happy

A Novel

LISA GRUNWALD

Random House Trade Paperbacks   New York

2006 Random House Trade Paperback Edition

Published in the United States by Random House Trade Paperbacks, an imprint of The Random House Publishing Group, a division of Random House, Inc., New York.

RANDOM HOUSE TRADE PAPERBACKS and colophon are trademarks of Random House, Inc.
READER'S CIRCLE and colophon are trademarks of Random House, Inc.

Originally published in hardcover in the United States by Random House, an imprint of The Random House Publishing Group, a division of Random House, Inc., in 2005.

Grateful acknowledgment is made to Probnoblem Music (BMI) for permission to reprint lyrics from "Don't Worry, Be Happy" by Bobby McFerrin.

LIBRARY OF CONGRESS CATALOGING-IN-PUBLICATION DATA
Grunwald, Lisa.
Whatever makes you happy: a novel / Lisa Grunwald.
p. cm.
ISBN 0-8129-7321-6
1. Middle-aged women—Fiction. 2. Midlife crisis—Fiction.
3. Married women—Fiction. 4. Happiness—Fiction.
5. Domestic fiction. lcsh I. Title.
PS3557.R837S43 2005
813'.54—dc22 2004061392

Printed in the United States of America

www.thereaderscircle.com

2 4 6 8 9 7 5 3 1

Book design by Dana Leigh Blanchette

For Stephen, my happy ending,
beginning, and middle

Whatever Makes
You Happy

1

If you're happy and you know it, clap your hands.
—*Old children's song*

When I was ten years old, my friends and I would sneak out at night and meet in our building's service courtyard to play spy games and exchange secrets. The courtyard was forbidden: it was dangerous; it was ominous. Purple shadows draped its brick walls like pieces of cast-off clothing. It was where the building sorted its trash and where God only knew what dangers lurked. It scared me into a hollow, cold silence, but I went anyway because I was in love with Michael Farber. He lived two floors below me, and I would have eagerly followed him into the heartless depths of a raging fire.

One night, near the dumpster, Michael found a blue plastic gem, a dime-sized circle with facets, like the kind that came in the gumball machines at the front of Woolworth's and Lamston's.

"A sapphire!" whispered Julian Becker, who lived three floors above me and was not the sharpest knife in the drawer.

"No, it's fake. It's only plastic," I told him.

"What?"

"You're such a dweeb," Michael said, with a certainty that Julian made no effort to contradict.

Julian was the extra boy, and Michael was the one I adored, the one who made me willing to brave my fears and the purple shadows.

"What are you going to do with it?" Michael asked me, putting it in my hand.

"Me?" I asked, flustered.

"You," he said.

"You're giving it to me?" I said.

"You could make it into a necklace."

Tenderly, appraisingly, he touched the chain I wore on my neck.

Then came the bang of a heavy door and the shuffle of heavy footsteps.

"Enemy spy!" Julian whispered, exultant, and pushed Michael into the corner behind the dumpster that served as our usual shield.

Standing alone, I shivered and froze.

"Come on, Sally!" Michael hissed from his hiding place.

"Quick, Sally!" Julian whispered.

But I was too terrified to move.

"Hide, Sally!" Michael shouted, and then, with a courage that would continue to move me for years and years to come, he emerged from his own safe hiding place and pulled me into the darkness behind an empty, discarded stove box.

"Who's that?" we heard a loud, harsh voice say.

The footsteps grew closer.

I clutched Michael's arm.

"Who's that at this time of night?" the voice said.

Michael put a finger to his lips.

Then the box was simply lifted away from us, as if a giant were moving a mountain. As we crouched, we stared up at a large black woman whose name was Posey Rivers and who was famous in the building for the flame-shaped scar on the back of her hand. Posey was the housekeeper for a family that didn't have any kids, but we'd seen her plenty of times, and she seemed to know all about us, too.

Under the purple shadows of this particular night, she gathered Michael and me into a hug against her huge, warm chest, which smelled, splendidly, of French fries.

"It's cold," she said. "You all must be chilly."

Neither of us said anything.

"November and not a coat on you all," Posey scolded. "Your mothers are going to catch a fit."

Michael and I looked at each other. Pressed against Posey's enormous breasts, we were finding it hard not to giggle.

"I'll bet *your* mama," Posey told me, "thinks you're downstairs at *his* place. And I'll be *his* mama thinks he's upstairs at *your* place."

Again, we didn't answer.

"Well, but Posey knew you were here," she said. She turned to shout over her shoulder. "And you can show your sorry face now, too, Julian Becker."

Timidly, Julian stepped out of hiding and grinned down at his feet.

"Oh, come on, I'm not going to bite you, Mr. Molasses," Posey said.

Julian stepped toward us, and there was something about the shy, dim look on his face that made Posey start to laugh. Posey's laugh was a hyuk-hyuk-hyuk affair, a tropical outburst every bit as big and broad as she was herself. And it wrapped around Michael and Julian and me with the sureness and strength of her arms, until all four of us were laughing together in the purple courtyard light.

In Posey's fragrant embrace, I felt the promise of Michael beside me, a promise both calming and thrilling; and I held and would cherish the blue plastic gem, a token that, three decades later, I would still keep in a pouch in my purse. I was safe—vibrantly, exquisitely safe—and for years to come, whenever I thought about happiness, this was the moment that would come, first and least self-consciously, to my mind.

2

I've got the bowl, the bone, the big yard.
I know I should be happy.
—*One dog to another in a*
Mike Twohy cartoon

*L*ying in bed with my husband one night, I am shocked to discover that I can't remember the size or shape of any other man's penis.

This alarms me, but in a quiet way, as one might be alarmed to discover that the ceiling plaster is starting to crack.

"The ceiling plaster is starting to crack," I say to Michael, because I suspect it is somewhat better than saying, "I can't remember the size or shape of any other man's penis."

It is a Wednesday night near the end of May, the traditional month when Manhattan springtime mingles with end-of-the-school-year shock. Between us, the bedspread stretches, broad and neat, like an unmapped country. Around us, the world is in order as well. Our daughters are now nine and ten years old, and shed somewhat fewer possessions in their travels around the apartment. The books on our shelves are alphabetized. No uncapped pens clutter up the desk. The stacks of clothes in our dresser drawers rise in tidy, specific piles.

"It looks like the Mojave Desert up there," I say, staring up at the ceiling.

"What?"

"It looks like the Mojave Desert."

To the left, over on his side of the bed, Michael cradles his favorite cereal bowl and clicks his teeth against the spoon with each precise yet slurpy bite. He looks up at the ceiling.

"Don't you think we should have it replastered?" I ask.

His eyes return to the TV screen, where the daily fortunes of New York's sports teams are unfolding in brisk succession.

"It's really starting to bug me," I say.

He turns to me now with a marital smile, a smile filled with wisdom and depraved acceptance, a smile that says: *You know that's not what it is.*

In fact, he is right, and I smile back, but I don't know what it is.

I suppose it might be the way he eats cereal.

Or the fact that, for the fourth night this week, the girls didn't fall asleep until ten, thus narrowing to Ginsu-knife thinness the slivers of time I can actually spend with him.

Or the fact that I didn't manage to get enough work done today on the book I am currently researching, a book that is called, not incidentally, *The History of Happiness* and is due, not incidentally, in three months.

Or it might be the Acme cartoon topography of tomorrow's to-do list, which includes glue-gunning a costume for Emily's school play, giving my editor an update on my book, starting in on the packing list for the girls' camp trunks, and whipping up a bowl of hummus for Katie's Ancient Egypt Day. I do not know how to make hummus, but I suspect that large amounts of mashing will be involved.

Let me hasten, really hasten, to say that I am not expecting the Fox 5 News Problem Solvers to show up at my door tonight. Or the Hundred Neediest Cases fund.

Still, if I've learned anything at all from the research I've done, it's that happiness has less to do with what people have than with what they think they want.

But do I know, even secretly, what it is that I think I want?

For years, researchers have been devising ever less intuitive methods for trying to quantify happiness. They have created all sorts of measures—known by acronyms, of course—such as the PWI, or Pleasure and Well-being Inventory, and the SWLS, or Satisfaction with Life Scale. Factors that have been weighed in the balance include racial tolerance, unemployment, frequency of sexual intercourse, number of television sets per capita, hours a week spent gardening, and belief in God. And yet with the exception of people living in extraordinary poverty or experiencing cataclysmic misfortune, there is remarkably little proof that any external factor has any lasting effect on the levels of personal happiness that people report.

Even Aristotle, who never stood on line at Zabar's and marveled at how it was possible to feel, simultaneously, so blessed by bounty and so insane with impatience; even Aristotle declared that happiness, to most people, was a constantly moving target. "Ordinary people," he wrote, "identify it with some obvious and visible good, such as pleasure or wealth or honor—some say one thing and some another, indeed very often the same man says different things at different times."

For the sick man, Aristotle said, happiness is health, and for the poor man it is riches.

And for the forty-year-old woman in bed with the forty-two-year-old man underneath the cracked ceiling plaster, happiness is, at the moment, only something she knows she should feel but for some dim reason can't.

I take Michael's dish to the kitchen for him and am sincerely trying to shake off my mood when the phone rings and the real fun begins.

"She's dead!" a familiar voice exults.

"Hi, Mom," I say.

"She's finally dead!"

I know without asking who the *she* has to be: Mom's tenant for the last seventeen years, a tenacious Austrian analyst who had worked and lived the last part of her life in the apartment where I spent the first part of mine—the apartment in whose shadowed courtyard Michael and I had long ago played.

My mother, living now in a retirement community in South Carolina, has never been hard-hearted enough to raise the doctor's rent. But she clearly is having no trouble now delighting in the woman's demise.

"You go check it out," she tells me excitedly.

"Okay, Mom."

"We've got to fix it up now."

"We?"

"I bet it's worth a fortune."

"And what are you going to do with the money you make? Bribe the nurses to smuggle in vodka?"

"Do this for me, won't you, baby?" my mother asks me plaintively, and of course I say yes, because requests that come from retirement homes are not requests but commandments.

"What do you think she did to the place?"

"Listen, I have to go, Mom," I say.

"Where?" she asks me petulantly.

"What do you mean, where? To bed, Mom," I say.

"It's only eleven-fifteen."

"Past my bedtime, Mom."

"You're not going to watch Leno?"

"Mom," I say.

"I'm sending you the keys," she says.

"Fine," I say.

"Federal Express," she adds pointedly, her unprecedented use of overnight shipping the clearest sign yet of her urgency.

There is nothing in the world like a conversation with my mother to make me want to fling my arms around Michael's shins.

"Your mom?" he asks when I come back to the bedroom.

"Of course," I say, climbing into bed.

"Let me guess. You never send her pictures of the kids."

"No."

"She bought Microsoft at seven twelve years ago."

"No."

"What, then?"

"Real news. The renter died."

Michael clicks off the television and looks at me warily. "And your mom's going to want you to handle it?"

I nod and pull the covers up to my chin.

I think about a purple light, a blue plastic gem, a courtyard. I think about the view from the window, the front hall closet, the bathroom tiles. I remember the walls of the hallway, which my father collaged with snapshots. Black-and-white for a few years, then color. A time tunnel, mosaicked by the past. I wonder if it is still there, or if the tenant painted over it, or had it scraped off the walls.

I know that my to-do list has just grown longer by countless items, but my mood is unaccountably brighter.

Michael sighs and gets up to follow his nighttime routine. I know the sounds so well. They are as mild and constant and comforting as the words of a lullaby: The eight squeaky steps across the old wood floor to the front door. The two snaps of the upper and lower locks. The twenty steps into the kitchen, all burners off, one light left on. The last look in at the girls, the redimming of their night-lights, which always, like an old worry, seem to grow stronger as the night wears on.

"Did the woman not have any family?" Michael asks me as he gets back into bed.

"Nope."

"So all this is on you?"

"It's okay," I say. "I can handle it."

I slide down between the sheets beside him, like a secret letter slipped into the safety of an envelope. And dream of ancient places, where everyone is young.

So this is how it's supposed to work in the mornings:

Up at 6:30, shower, coffee, wake the girls, make them breakfast, kiss Michael good-bye at the door, take the girls downstairs to the bus, come back up, drink coffee, make beds, read the paper, put up the laundry, and sit back down to work.

To which I can only respond: Oh, please.

If it works that way one morning in ten, it's time for my own private Mardi Gras.

This morning, Mom calls at seven.

"Did you get the keys yet?"

"Mom," I say, pulling on some jeans. "It's seven o'clock in the morning."

"I know. But I sent the package by the Federal Express."

My mother has a tendency to overuse the definite article.

"Federal Express, Mom. Not *the* Federal Express."

"They told me it would be overnight."

"It'll get here. It's not supposed to come until ten."

"You call me when it comes."

"Mom."

"Call me."

By the time I hang up, the girls, hair unbrushed and possibly unbrushable, are engaged in an apartment-wide hunt for Katie's baseball cap; the unsweetened, rejected cereals from the Kellogg's variety pack are all I can offer for breakfast; and Michael is probably already taking his first patient's pulse before I realize he's gone.

The girls and I sprint to the corner.

"Don't forget my costume!" Emily shouts from the window of the school bus, her hair slipstreaming into the air behind her as she turns to resume her seat.

The girls' morning departure usually provides me a moment of light liberation, and I mean to go quickly back upstairs to work. But instead I find myself standing to watch as their school bus pulls out and moves down the street. The large yellow rectangle shrinks until, like a tiny knot on a long thread, it is woven into the city's fabric. Something like fear overtakes me, a hint of the separation to come. The girls will be going to sleepaway camp for the very first time this summer, and I will be left with Michael and a nonfiction search for happiness that I'll have no excuse to avoid.

The play is *You're a Good Man, Charlie Brown,* and Emily has the part of Lucy, and I have been asked to provide something little-girlish, preferably with polka dots. Since inspiration struck a week or so ago, and I retrieved an old pregnancy shirt from the recesses of my closet, all I've done is put some pins in the hem. Back upstairs, I plug in the glue gun, without which I believe Manhattan motherhood itself would dissolve, and I heat up my coffee and settle down to work at the kitchen table.

Our walls could use a good paint job, and someday it would be nice to redo the cabinets, but the kitchen is in order, and that is not an insignificant fact. The kitchen is the largest room in our typically cramped Upper West Side apartment and is wired just well enough to support the necessary appliances for a mother and wife and freelance writer at the start of the new millennium. With its array of humming machines—aging PowerBook on the warped butcher-block table, fax and copier, scanner and printer, dishwasher and washing machine—the kitchen has in effect become the command post, the conning tower, of the vessel that I steer every day, despite the changing climate and occasionally uncharted waters.

On the walls are my children's drawings, representing a host of styles and ages and who knows what budding resentments. On the counter is the costume. Also the latest chapter of my book. On the bulletin board is the calendar—cramped and colorful—with the milestones of a Manhattan spring laid out like the squares on a board game. Ancient Egypt Day. Field Day. Picnic. The play. The book fair, where I'm a cashier. And Michael's hospital benefit. And my best friend's sister's wedding.

The spring sun throws a shimmering rectangle of light on the kitchen wall. At my elbow, an old measuring cup brims with a bouquet of colored markers.

Carefully, I drip an indelible line of hot glue beside the pins on the polka-dot shirt and then fold back the fabric to make a hem. Strangely, I am shortening this shirt so that my little girl—who did not yet have a name the first time I wore it—will be able to *look* like a little girl when she plays the part onstage. And more strangely still, when I am finished and I've put the glue gun away and taken the shirt to the girls' bedroom, I stop and press it to my cheek. That is not one of my usual moves, and for the second time today, I find myself wondering what's gotten into me—or what's being taken away.

But Jimmy Shannon, my editor, is expecting my call this morning for a full update on my book. My book is supposed to be about how the concept of happiness has evolved from the moral standards of ancient Greece to the self-help books, Paxil prescriptions, and feng shui floor plans of today.

Here is what I've got so far:

I've got one chapter on the early Greek concepts of happiness and another on the idea of happiness as an American right.

I've got articles from professional journals ranging in topic from philosophy to marketing to mood drugs to God. "Hedonic Level of Affect." "The Biochemical Aspects of Joy."

I've got pictures and, in some cases, samples of a host of now-defunct products: a Happiness bicycle seat from the 1890s, a balding cure from the 1910s, a flatware pattern from the 1940s, a board game from the 1960s, a hair dye from the 1970s ("Just foam Happiness® into your hair"), and a Happiness toothbrush—I found it on eBay but don't know its vintage—with two plastic breasts where the bristles should be.

I've got appointments to interview one clinical psychologist who is trying to prove that happiness is a genetic trait, another who studies addiction, and a peppy Boston woman who runs a place called the Laughter Institute.

I've got transcripts from speeches given at England's University of Birmingham for the annual Happiness Lectures, a series endowed, in all earnestness, a quarter of a century ago.

None of which—witness last night in bed—has gotten me any closer to a permanent grasp of the concept. But hey, the day is young.

Jimmy has told me to call him at exactly nine, but at exactly nine I am surfing the Web for hummus recipes, discovering, to my great dismay, that I should already have been soaking chickpeas in water for an entire night. So when the phone rings at a quarter past, it's Jimmy, sounding wounded.

"Cookie!" he scolds when he hears my voice. "Why do you keep me waiting?"

This is a quaint echo of our long, erratic, savage romance. It seems that, nearly twenty years later, he is still most compelled by the absence of me.

I try now to remember what Jimmy looked like naked, and I startle myself by succeeding.

"Cookie! When do I see some glorious pages?" he asks. His voice still cajoles: shameless, British, and naughty.

The History of Happiness was his idea, the fourth in a series I've written for him. My first was called *The History of Anger* and was an unexpected hit, principally because its publication coincided with O. J. Simpson's arrest. *The History of Jealousy* followed, also a big success, probably because it coincided with O. J. Simpson's trial. And then, two years ago, came *The History of Love,* which absolutely bombed. Despite my worst fear—that people only want to read the history of unpleasant emotions—Jimmy has been insistent that I try happiness next. The fact that the Dalai Lama has published a bestselling book called *The Art of Happiness* does not deter him but rather leads him to believe that the subject has legs—albeit legs covered by a long orange gown.

Now and then, he'll call to give me updates on the numbers.

"The Lama is holding steady," he'll say.

"How am I going to compete with the Dalai Lama?" I'll ask.

"Oh, you're going to leave him in the dust."

"I'm going to leave the Dalai Lama in the dust?" I'll say.

"Bury him," Jimmy will say.

And periodically he will call to ask for new pages.

"I'm not ready yet," I tell him now.

"Don't be absurd! I haven't seen anything new in three months! You'll come in next Thursday."

I rub my forehead. "Not next week, Jimmy," I say. "It's May. It's the end of the school year."

"Ah," he says. "The chicklets."

"And my mother just unloaded her old apartment on me."

"I'll be sure to tell Barnes and Noble."

We compromise with Wednesday, June fourth.

"Remember," Jimmy says. "There will be a quiz. The subject is happiness. Hit the books."

✳

And I do hit the books. Or, more accurately, the Internet. At the Columbia University website, I call up the library search engine.

SEARCH FOR . . . and in the space, I type the word *happiness*.

Search for happiness.

I laugh to myself.

I push the SUBMIT button and watch the browser's icon turn.

I read:

Happiness
Search also under:
Cheerfulness
Contentment
Joy
Mental Health
Pleasure

Is this a recipe? Or a menu? Or neither? Are these synonyms? Or not quite?

I find myself staring at the word *joy*. I let it conjure for me. It calls up the days on which my children were born, and the day on which I married. *Joy* summons up arrows of light bouncing off waves on Cape Cod, and the feeling I get when I open our front door after a long time away.

And then *pleasure*. The word invokes vanilla ice cream over hot blueberry pie, and diving into a swimming pool on a scorching day, and having Michael, ten years into our marriage, intently, and for the first time, kiss the back of my left calf.

Mental health. Could I come back to that one?

And *cheerfulness*? That is, perhaps, Michael's most special talent, with all his days of endless patience and goodwill toward men—and toward marriage.

But *contentment*. Is that happiness? Or is that only resignation wearing a funny hat?

I work, making notes of more books to pursue, for at least half an hour.

The Federal Express guy rings the doorbell at exactly ten o'clock and bestows on me, in one tidy gesture, the keys to my mother's apartment and a dusty and dangerous summer.

3

Well, if I can't be happy, I can be useful, perhaps.
—*Louisa May Alcott*

At its very best, the apartment in which I grew up possessed a certain bohemian charm. What my parents lacked in good furniture they generally made up for in decorative flair. What they lacked in marital harmony they generally made up for in aesthetic accord. When I was a child, the apartment housed numerous collections, among them half a dozen large, framed vintage posters, as many antique grocery-store signs, various jars filled with Cape Cod seashells and beach glass, and a prismatic array of flea-market pitchers, filled with the flowers that Dad always hung up, prematurely, to dry.

By eleven, the city streets are balmy and fine, and despite the needling from Jimmy, I walk to Mom's apartment with unexpected brio. My old building, which is sandwiched between two grander ones on Central Park West, is just at the edge of our neighborhood, and so I have passed it many times, especially heading east through the park, or visiting my friend T.J., who happens to live on Central Park West too. Today, though, Mom's building is my actual destination, and I find myself stopping at the entrance to examine the fluted column that I used to play on every morning, waiting for my school bus. There wasn't much of a game. I would stand on the column's base and try to move from corner to corner without falling off. In the days when my father still waited with me, he'd find some reason to look away while I climbed behind the column, and then he'd call my name, pretending that he thought I'd disappeared.

"Don't scare me like that!" he would say as I would pop out from my not quite hiding place to see the mock relief on his face.

Standing by the column now, I remember my giddy pleasure at the pretense of his glee.

It has been twenty-one years since his death, and nearly twenty since I have had any reason to enter this building. What I discover when I do is that our once comfortable, not to say seedy, West Side apartment house has been transmuted by time and pretension and faux-marbling techniques. Gold-painted griffins now frolic on the ceiling. Tapestry-like panels hang grandly from high wrought-iron bars.

I know the elevator buttons, the elevator door. Upstairs, the floor has been recarpeted, but the smell is exactly the same: it is the hallway smell of Jewish cooking, ammonia, and stale, trapped seasons.

At the front door, I find myself fumbling for Mom's package. The note she's tucked in with the keys is hatcheted by her underlines:

SALLY. <u>PLEASE</u> GO OVER <u>FIRST</u> THING, AND <u>CALL</u> ME AS <u>SOON</u> AS YOU GET <u>THERE</u>.

I know the view of the park from the seventh-floor window; the single L-shaped bathroom that I shared with my parents for all those years; the smell of my mother's lavender soap; the safety of the locked front door; the chipped wood floor by the dining room table; the wide living room with the low radiator that steamed up the windows in winter.

Quickly, I turn the key in the lock and step inside the apartment. The lights are off, and a person has died here, so it's just a little bit spooky. For a moment, I feel that I might turn the lights on and find myself tumbling into the past.

It turns out that that's only partly true. Time has clearly frozen here. But it has frozen several times, so wandering through the rooms is like discovering successive strata in a rocky plateau, and the bottom layer—the layer I knew—is not immediately visible.

Riotous flowered wallpaper covers the hall where Dad's collages once were. But that is only one manifestation of the doctor's apparently madcap style. Here, in the front half of the apartment, where she must have seen her patients, is 1920s Vienna, with leather couch, kilim rugs, crystal sconces, and dusty books. Here, in the back rooms, is 1970s Museum Gift Shop: plaster cherubs, heroes, and winged horses overwhelm the bathroom and hall. Our two small bedrooms have been combined into one, and a small Venus de Milo is perched there before a gray, stained mirror, looking particularly mournful. This room also features a single bed, a medicinal smell, a box of rubber gloves, a digital clock that looks as if it was among the first ones manufactured, and a series of clip-on lamps that were obviously less and less successful in warding off the encroaching darkness.

I wander, holding my breath somewhat—as if it is water around me, not air—back out into the front room. One of my parents' large framed posters still hangs above the fireplace. It is a poster that I stared at often and remember well: it always confused me when I was a child. The poster advertised a French house paint called Nitrolian and showed a painter covering some steps with red paint while holding a can of paint that showed a painter covering some steps with red paint while holding a can, and so on.

The chaos of the apartment, however, makes the poster look simple by comparison. In this room alone, there are five separate bookshelves—of varying depths, widths, heights, colors, and textures. A manual pencil sharpener is bolted to a windowsill. A paper cutter with a rusty, raised blade is perched on a rusted blue file cabinet. A half dozen other file cabinets offer a haphazard history of twentieth-century office design. In the kitchen, two round fluorescent lights converse with each other in buzzes and blinks.

Back in the office, I look through dusty windows out onto Central Park, where a flock of pigeons circles the playground, just as the birds did when I was a child. I can feel my father's presence, and the ache that goes with it. I sit. I try not to feel too much. But I am dizzy with the past.

Absentmindedly, I open the nearest file cabinet, which is labeled "A–C." Inside, I find perhaps a dozen files, a bunch of loose pennies, several dozen paper clips, and a few balled-up receipts.

In the second file cabinet, mercurially labeled "A–D," I find more files, some pens, scissors, pencils, more pennies, a hammer, a florist's smoky green vase, and a file folder filled with blank notepads.

Reflexively, I scoop up the pennies, place them in a dish on a corner of the desk, add the first drawer's pennies to them, grab a pad, and get to work seeing which pens still write and which ones don't. I don't know why I do this, but I find it somehow calming.

I scribble meaningless zigzag lines across the slightly yellowed paper, wondering when these pens were last used, and what words, if any, they wrote. Fifteen minutes pass this way in still and musty silence, and in the silence, I recognize something I haven't felt for years: the nearly exotic, potent blend of privacy and youth.

"Why didn't you call me?" my mother asks when, coming back into my own apartment, I pick up the ringing telephone.

"The phone's been disconnected," I tell her, and in fact it probably has been. But in truth I completely forgot to call her once I was in the apartment.

"You could have called from your cell," she says.

"I know, Mom," I say. "I'm sorry."

"But you went?"

"Of course I went."

"And?"

And so I tell her what a mess the place is. I describe the cherubs, the file cabinets, the rust, the dust, the chaos.

"This is a huge amount of work," I say.

"Oh, you can do anything, baby," she says, which may seem like a compliment but is actually more like a threat.

"You know, Mom," I say, "in my spare time, I'm actually trying to write a book."

"What do you think the apartment would go for?" she asks, with the kind of zealous indifference to my professional life that I've always found too exhausting to fight.

"It's smaller than I remembered," I say.

"Things look bigger to children."

"Didn't this woman have any family?" I ask, even though I know the answer.

"None," Mom says. "But thank goodness I do."

"Mom," I say. "Are you happy?"

"Happy? Sure."

"What makes you happy?"

"Happy?"

"Yes."

"What makes me happy?"

"Yes."

"It would make me happy if you would do the apartment."

"No, I mean really, Mom," I say.

"Are you getting deep?" my mother asks, as if *deep* is a synonym for *itchy*.

"Sometimes," I say, "I just feel, I don't know—"

"What?"

Sad? Confused? Nostalgic? Lost?

Did she ever lie in bed with my father and try to remember other men? Had there been other men to remember?

"What?" she says again, and I shake off this rogue impulse to tell her what I'm actually feeling. Nothing good ever comes from that.

"It's a lot, you know," I say instead. "With the kids. And with the book."

"The kids are going to be at the camp. You'll have nothing but time on your hands," she says.

The kids. The camp. The time on my hands. It occurs to me that there is a camp packing list and that I haven't purchased a shoelace. This is my barely convincing rationale for a thinly disguised diversion. Truth is, the trunks will not be picked up for another month, but the simplicity of following someone else's to-do list seems suddenly alluring. And so, burying my happiness research beneath the Camp Sha-no-Wah handbook, I opt for an online shopping spree, and—bypassing an ad for the perfume Clinique Happy (slogan: "choose happiness")—I load things by twos into the virtual shopping cart, pausing only to consider colors and sizes and openability of bottles and tubes. Katie and Emily have had plenty of nights away from home but never more than one at a time.

I contemplate the packing list, which is really a delicate ode to all the things that can go wrong. Bug bites, bee stings, sunburns, blisters, headaches, head colds, and let's not forget lice. I've had eleven years of doing the maintenance work on my girls' bodies. It is both liberating and harrowing to imagine them doing it all themselves. What are the chances, for example, that Katie will suddenly learn that hair brushed on Monday doesn't "last" until Wednesday? I will probably be brought up on charges by the maternal court if I don't insist on radical, camp-friendly haircuts. But the girls will surely resist this, and my insisting will make them miserable, and on the eve of our first long separation, I want no more sadness than necessary.

Which brings up a question for my book: How necessary is sadness to the experience of bliss?

But I don't have time to pursue this, because I have to clean the broccoli.

T.J. calls as I'm seasoning the chicken.

"Where were you this morning?" she asks, clearly offended, as she always is when people are not where she wants them to be.

In fairness, we do talk nearly every morning, usually when she's on her way to work, and sometimes when she's just gotten there. Occasionally, there are lunchtime calls, too. Though I am a book writer and T.J. is a book editor, our work rarely makes the list of topics. More commonly, we discuss children, parents, babysitters, neighborhood bargains, shared acquaintances, schools, clothes, marriage, sex, recipes, childhood ailments, and her sister's upcoming wedding. After twenty years of friendship that began in the tossed salad of a monthly magazine, we have more confidences between us than we can accurately recall. And if we also have more contests, we are much slower to admit it.

Recently, for example, in a rare confessional moment, T.J. put me in charge of counting how many weeks it's been since Ethan, her husband, was able to make love to her. As a matter of fact, it's been nearly two months, but she doesn't really want to know this, let alone to remember that I do. T.J.'s desire to be and seem wildly successful makes it hard for her to admit things, even to me, in any consistent way.

"I need you to look at two dresses," she says now.

"Why? When?"

"*Yesterday.* My sister is driving me crazy. First she said I could wear any navy blue dress I wanted, but now she's insisting on floor length, and so, well, I've got it narrowed down to two."

"What does Ethan say?" I ask her.

"Ethan wouldn't notice if I left the house dressed as a crossing guard."

"I'm really swamped," I say. "Mom's renter died," I tell her.

"Swamped?" T.J. repeats with a bit of a snort. She is still at her office, packing up, and she's shouting into her speaker phone. Telling T.J. I'm swamped is always a calculated risk, because no one can ever be more swamped than she is. She's simply too busy running the hottest young imprint in publishing and looking over her shoulder to make sure that no one's gaining on her and looking ahead to see who she wants to catch.

"So I went to look at the place—" I begin.

"Oh, that's where you were. And?"

"And it's a mess."

"Of course it's a mess."

"But the view. You know. Well, it's *your* view," I say. "I mean, it's your view but smaller."

"The view isn't smaller," T.J. says pointedly. "What's smaller is the number of windows that you can see the view from."

"You sound like a broker."

"You know, I'm pretty sure Reese Witherspoon has an apartment in that building."

"Really."

"Is your mom going to sell it?"

"She wants to."

"I bet she could get a ton for it."

"Who knows?"

"Are you going to have to deal with it?"

"What do you think?"

"So, hire someone," she says, which is pretty much her answer to everything—from extra copy editors and cover designers to personal trainers for her children.

"I can't afford to," I say. "And anyway, Mom wants me to do it."

"Pay for it from the sale," she says.

"T.J. This was my childhood apartment."

She laughs. "So, what's your point?" she says.

"You have absolutely no sentiment," I say.

"No," she says. "I just have no time."

"You're so lucky," I say to Michael that night, which, given the fact that he has just described a day in which he had to hospitalize two patients and nearly lost one, is a pretty ridiculous thing to say.

We laugh. It is a good, long, up-on-our-elbows-in-bed-married-talking laugh. It is the kind of laugh that we usually have only after the best kind of sex, and indeed, I put the girls to bed early tonight, and I took a shower, and I smoothed my skin with lotion, and I seduced my husband, and I felt the strenuous joy of his orgasm, and a fair one of my own.

"Why, then, exactly, am I lucky?" he asks.

"You know. Your parents."

"Um, sweetie, my parents are dead," he says.

I laugh. "You know that's not what I mean," I tell him. "I mean, that they sold your apartment."

He kisses my shoulder and tucks a stray strand of hair behind my ear.

"Well, your mom is going to sell this one."

"But it's going to be such a bitch to sort through. To clean up. To organize—"

"Why?" he asks, in a slightly menacing tone.

"Why what?"

"Why do you have to do all this?"

"Because she's old and she asked me to," I say.

Michael pauses, clearly doing battle with conflicting impulses: the impulse to diagnose, the impulse to hold off treatment.

"Sweetheart," he finally says. "You know you do have a book to write."

"I know."

"And two children who—"

"Are going to sleepaway camp."

"Not till the end of June!" he says.

"They'll be gone," I say and realize, as I say it, that it's actually going to happen.

"I'm just going to ask you one question," he says. "Do you really think you need something else?"

A note for *The History of Happiness:*

Almost all the people I know, almost all the time I have known them, have thought that they needed something else.

Michael and I watch the news. Suicide rates are up among teens. Parts of Georgia are flooded. Eight more cases of West Nile virus have been reported. I should be happy that I don't have a suicidal teenager, don't live in Georgia, don't have West Nile virus. Michael eats his cereal. I should be happy that we have cereal, milk, bowls, spoons. Teeth. I slip down into the sheets as Michael gets up to check the locks and turn off the lights and get back into bed.

The room is dark and suddenly foreign.

He lies beside me like a parallel line.

"I love you," he says in the darkness.

"I love you, too," I answer wistfully, amazed that in mere moments, this love—which is marital, practical, solid—has completely wiped out the fizz of sex.

"If you really want to do the apartment—"

"I don't see another way," I say tartly, but I'm not being really honest with him.

In fact I decided to take on the apartment the moment I stepped into it alone. The apartment is a Pandora's box, and for me, the mess it has spilled out seems every bit as irresistible as sin.

4

Nothing is more fatal to happiness than
the remembrance of happiness.
—*André Gide*

*A*ncient Egypt Day dawns bright and buoyant, but slightly behind schedule. At a quarter to eight, the girls run for the bus, Katie
clutching her plastic container of hummus in one hand and the
basis of her caftan—the inevitable "old white sheet from home"—
in the other.

I know of no one—not even T.J.—who has a linen closet large
enough to house the inventory of old white sheets that a couple
of grade-school springtimes demand. But keeping old white sheets
around for makeshift caftans is something I genuinely consider to
be a perk of motherhood. Arts and crafts. Colored markers. Good
strong paper. Well-shucked crayons. I love being the kind of mother

whose orange Elmer's glue tops close and open without having to be snipped off or stabbed. I love making sure the girls have enough socks, and loose-leaf paper, and hair elastics. I know all this is part of the collective modern fantasy that, by doing our jobs a certain way, parents can actually form and shape our children as we wish. But the truth is that I love, just as much, the me that having my girls has shaped: the me that is solid, strong, ready.

This was, actually, one of the miscalculations of my life: the extent to which I would not just welcome, but crave, the role of mother. I hadn't planned on this, just as I hadn't planned on falling in love with my children as wildly as I have. I didn't imagine that getting embraced, or getting tickled, or getting begged for a bedtime story could ever compete with getting published, or getting invited, or getting laid.

But it did compete, and it still does. For my children, I have given up smoking, given up office hours, given up unplugged phones and all sorts of other things that might make it easier to write. For them, I have ventured into the tropical rain forest of modern pharmacology, where—in pursuit of the even temper that nicotine used to provide me and that modern life constantly menaces—I have sampled the fruits of the Paxil, Zoloft, and Zyban trees (though at the moment, I stand gratefully in a chemical-free clearing).

And why? Mainly so that I can enjoy the show. Mainly so that I will be there, really *be there,* at the end of the day, when Katie walks through the front door wearing a tilting sun-god headdress and carrying a long fan made from a yardstick, paper plates, and paper feathers. Mainly so that I will be there when she falls to her knees before Emily, fans her with solemn devotion, and intones the words "Hello, Great One."

The afternoon light will be strong and warm, and we will laugh together while her eyes, still so large and puppyish, shine, and her eyelashes shoot from them like the sun's rays.

❋

In the meantime, however, I've got T.J. on my back.

"You are coming over now," she declares on the phone when I come back upstairs.

"Why aren't you on your way to work?"

"Because you are coming over now."

Twenty minutes later, T.J. opens her front door for me and stands in a satin bathrobe, looking better than any forty-year-old has any right to look.

I am also forty. But while I, even on a good day, tend to look forty-five, T.J., even on a bad day, tends to look thirty-five. Some of this is inherited, and some of it has been purchased. Personal trainers, nutritionists, dermatologists, makeup consultants, hair colorists, and eyebrow shapers: All of them have contributed, at one time or another, to the generally stunning effect. But then, there are also her temple-high cheekbones. Her broad shoulders. And her faultless lips, which form an almost perfect heart whenever she is smiling.

At the moment, she is not.

"Morning," I say. Then: "What?"

"I'm in a rush," she says.

I follow her past the kitchen, where Alice, the youngest of her three children, is screaming *Don't! Don't! Don't! No!* while her babysitter sings off-key and tries vainly to feed her.

"Need to go to her?" I ask T.J.

"No. She's fine," T.J. says—all evidence to the contrary.

So we continue our journey down the apartment's lengthy hallway, where doors always seem, cartoonlike, to be opening and shutting on surprising new forms of chaos. We pass the laundry room, where the spinning washer is shaking so hard that it looks as if it's about to waddle across the floor. We pass the maid's room, where the maid, Bernadette, has just returned from taking T.J.'s older children to school. We pass the guest room, where the wallpaper has recently been removed and a man in coveralls—poised to replace it with something more perfect—is perched like a cat on the top of a ladder. Then T.J.'s study, where the desk ripples with stacked books and manuscripts, and then her husband's, where Ethan waves and smiles to us with opaque, distracted goodwill.

In the decade that has passed since they married, T.J.'s success as a publisher has been directly proportional to Ethan's failure as an entrepreneur. Ethan is a huge failure, a dramatic failure, a continuing saga of failure in which each chapter is framed by a new idea. Ethan has ideas the way that some people have accidents. Among his greatest hits have been a restaurant that served exclusively breakfast at night, a travel magazine for New York City residents alone, and a landscape gardening business for Manhattan rooftops. He tried to sell—as gourmet beverages—bottled rainwater from different parts of the world. He backed a Broadway musical so disastrously bad that the *New York Times* critic wrote his review not about the show but about the nature of failure.

These days, I know from T.J., Ethan has been spending an inordinate amount of time in his study, surfing the Web. He makes plans for vacations she will never have time to take, reads want ads for jobs he will never be moved to apply for, eavesdrops on chat rooms, dabbles on eBay, takes IQ tests, and searches for the national zeitgeist as if it is the Holy Grail.

Passing his desk, T.J. waves back to him cheerfully and, once inside the bedroom, pulls the door closed, casually shutting out all chances of further contact with him.

No. He's fine, T.J. would say. All evidence to the contrary.

Behind her, the king-sized bed shimmers, a five-hundred-thread-count Egyptian cotton island. Even rumpled Porthault sheets look expensive, I think—or maybe their opulence simply reflects my knowledge that it is T.J.'s maid, not T.J., who will make the bed.

On her bedside table is a row of thick, colored candles.

"Those are new," I say.

"Aromatherapy," she replies.

I actually saw these online at one point:

Wishes do come true with "Happiness," a fresh and exhilarating floral fragrance that vibrantly scents any room. Whether you are seeking the happiness from the sun's warmth or the happiness of a fairy-tale ending, just blow out your candle and make a wish.

With the help of her ample salary, T.J. is always pursuing the latest of life's enhancements, not only of her appearance but also of her experiences: down mattress pads for better sleep, center-orchestra tickets for better entertainment, sixteen-year-old single-malt Scotch for better oblivion, and private Pilates lessons for better relaxation or, as the banner I saw at a street fair put it:

FITNESS IS THE FIRST REQUISITE TO HAPPINESS.
—*Joseph Pilates*

T.J. is addicted to ever new forms of comfort while oblivious to the need they might reveal; she works so hard that she doesn't enjoy about eighty percent of her life; she is married to a man who seems to lack both professional and sexual aim; she runs from her children whenever she can. And still, she's fine, they're fine, he's fine. What evidence to the contrary? For T.J., it's simply an article of faith that happiness will be the natural by-product of success.

Every two years or so, she has a crisis of some sort, and ends up having a panic attack and drinking Scotch in a bathtub and crying to me on the phone. But invariably, she somehow ends up getting another promotion, or landing another huge author, or being named to some panel, or appearing on *Larry King Live* to talk about the global impact of Harry Potter or electronic publishing. And despite the undeniable jealousy that all that can inspire in me, I find something almost infinitely touching about her striving anyway. Sensing the chaos on the other side of the door right now, and looking at the burnt-out matches that lie beside her candles, I am reminded—not for the first time—that T.J.'s brand of happiness, for all its extravagance, is no more dependable than my own.

One of the dresses is Armani. The other one is Anne Klein. They are virtually identical: sleeveless, simple, navy, floor length, silky, elegant, fine. One of them has a scoop neck, and the other a V. But T.J. models them for me, in turn, with an air of portent, and I try to see a difference and embrace a choice.

"And what are you going to wear?" she asks, slipping a pair of stockings on, now that she is dressing for work.

"I have no idea," I say.

"The wedding's in less than a week," she says.

"She's your sister, not mine," I say. "No one will care what I'm wearing."

"Not if you don't," she says, stepping into shoes that she'd never wear if she had to walk, and not be driven, to work.

I put the dress she's returning back into its garment case.

"So what about the apartment?" she asks, now facing her dressing table and her face.

"I was thinking I'd go over there now," I say. "Why don't you come?"

She laughs as if no more absurd suggestion has ever been made.

"Uh, remember work?" she says.

"I have to work, too," I say.

"So why are you going there?"

"I told you," I said, picking up my purse. "I'm cleaning it up for my mom."

"Remind me what the next one's supposed to be called, anyway," T.J. says merrily. *"The History of Procrastination?"*

"I'm glad I amuse you," I say, which is a lie.

❋

I stand outside T.J.'s apartment building, transfixed by the usual tangle of shoulds. I should go home, should work on the book, should go to Mom's, should put up some laundry.

Mom's apartment wins.

Today, a handyman is bundling newspapers near the service stairs by the front elevator. His face is dark brown and sweaty, and he hums "The Battle Hymn of the Republic," or something that sounds a lot like it. I nod and smile anonymously.

Then he stops whistling, cocks his head to one side, and says: "You going up to 7B?"

"How'd you know that?" I ask.

"Know everyone in the building," he says. "Figured if you were a stranger, you'd be going up there."

"I'm Sally Farber," I say, extending my hand. "My mother owns the apartment."

"Robert," he says, with a slight nod to the red script stitched on his blue coveralls. "Need any help?" he asks pleasantly.

"Who doesn't?" I say.

I hear him laughing softly as the elevator door closes, and the laugh, though so much quieter than hers, reminds me of Posey. So I push the B button for basement, and I get out in the gray-walled maze of corridors and steam pipes that leads out back, to the service courtyard, which is tiny and dirty and unhallowed: paved in cracked concrete, walled in by barbed wire and chain links and shadows.

I search, mentally, for Michael and briefly find his childhood face, but not the face I saw this morning—or rather, the face I failed to see through my current haze of hummus and self-doubt.

Upstairs, the apartment seethes with summer heat and years of dust. I note only one air conditioner—an enormous one in the front room—but its cord is conspicuously frayed, and it isn't plugged in, and I'm not going to try it.

"Air Conditioner," I write in a notebook that I find in one of the file cabinets. The pencil I take from the doctor's desk is one of those old-fashioned gray ones, with the flat, gold-banded erasers.

I go to the kitchen to check for cleaning supplies and find only a few cans of pasty Ajax, a bottle of Ivory liquid, and some chewed-up sponges. A rusted Brillo pad sits like a toadstool in the corner of the sink, which is clothed in a stained, limp, floral skirt. The glass-windowed cabinets are nearly opaque with grime. The countertops are still covered in the orange linoleum that my father used to say was the color of poppies and my mother used to say was the color of lox. The linoleum tiles on the floor are new, though: a ghastly faux-wood check pattern that would look awful even if the wood were real. Near the sink, I can't help but notice, the corners of several tiles have already peeled up, and I'm pretty sure that what lies beneath them is the smoky blue cloud pattern of the old kitchen tiles, and before I know it, I have sat down beside the kitchen sink and, with nothing more than the doctor's pencil and an ancient pair of poultry shears, I am tearing up the faux-wood linoleum, digging down to the floor whose only greater beauty is the beauty of the past.

According to Annie Modesitt, author of a book about the how-tos and wherefores of knitting, "There is a strong connection between our ability to use our hands in useful work, and our ability to find happiness in daily life." Indeed, Modesitt believes deeply in what she calls the "daily, repetitive tasks" and writes longingly of "the compulsive calmness that infuses our pedestrian chores with poetry."

For at least three solid hours, with a break only to look in vain for garbage bags, I build a low fortress of faux-wood tiles around me. Compulsive calmness indeed. When I was quitting smoking, I did this sort of thing all the time: jigsaw puzzles, crossword puzzles, needlepoint, knitting, solitaire. They are all forms of self-hypnosis, I think, and they make me dreamy and blank.

Today is a Friday, and the girls get out of school early, but they both happen to have playdates, and I know that Frieda (our once full-time, now sometime sitter) will be picking them up.

At around three in the afternoon, my cell phone starts to ring, but I figure that it's just my mother, checking up on me yet again, and so I do not answer.

It is not until the third or fourth call that I realize—more like remember—that there might be other people who may want to get in touch with me.

My legs stiff and my poultry-shears hand slightly blistered, I walk into the living room and dig my phone out of my handbag. Somehow I am surprised to find that it's Michael who is calling.

"When are you coming home?" he asks.

"Home?"

I realize that I'm slightly spellbound.

"Sweetheart?"

"Sorry."

"Soon?" he says.

"Sure," I say, bringing the phone with me back to the kitchen.

"Because the girls and I would kind of like to see you," Michael says.

"It's a mess here," I say, peeling up another chunk of linoleum, enjoying the satisfying *thwuck* of the adhesive letting go.

"What are you doing?" he says.

"Mostly just taking inventory," I say, grabbing hold of a particularly big piece of tile, which comes off nearly in one piece.

"Inventory?"

"What do they call that, in the emergency room, when you're trying to figure out what patient goes first?"

"Triage?"

"Yeah, triage. Well, that's what I've got to do here."

"Except it's furniture, not people."

"Yes, honey, I'm aware of that."

"Well, how about if the girls and I come up there and help you?"

"No!" I hear myself shout. A little too quickly. A little too harshly. And a little bit too much as if there's already some kind of secret that I'm trying to protect.

5

I've learned from experience that the greater part of
our happiness or misery depends on our dispositions
and not on our circumstances.
—*Martha Washington*

At the forefront of a new wave of thinking on the subject of happiness is a forty-six-year-old psychologist by the name of Stanley Ellis. Dr. Ellis does his research—and occasionally gives well-attended lectures—at New York University. There, for the last decade or so, he has been attempting to find empirical proof for a theory that, if correct, could drive whole industries into oblivion and whole marriages into the ground.

The theory—which has been propounded by a variety of psychologists—is that all human beings are born with a kind of emotional set point, a level of happiness that can shift in a lifetime by small degrees but that, absent a cataclysmic event, will stay pretty much unchanged.

Scientists such as Dr. Ellis have borrowed this term, *set point,* from the world of nutrition, where, in a number of well-documented and deeply depressing experiments, other researchers have more or less proven that no matter what a person's weight loss might be on any given diet, that person is destined by genetic makeup to revert to a certain weight, a set point. In other words: Once a chubbo, always a chubbo.

On Monday morning—as per the arrangement I made when in full denial about the mayhem of May—I meet Dr. Ellis in his office.

Short, bespectacled, and genial, he shakes my hand and shows me an eight-foot-long bulletin board, where innumerable graphs and charts and articles hang behind him leafily. I note graphs called "Contentment by Gender," "Contentment by Income," "Subjective Experience of Success vs. Occupation," "Happiness by Marriage," "Longevity vs. Joy."

Despite the metaphysical, not to say goofy, sound of some of these graphs, they are mathematically and statistically complex, and Dr. Ellis clearly delights in their obvious elegance. At the same time, when I inform him that I'm mathematically obtuse, he has no trouble cutting to the chase.

"Happy people," he says, "seem basically to be happy people, whatever their circumstances. Unhappy people seem basically to be unhappy people, whatever their circumstances."

My grandmother used to put this another way: *Happy is as happy does.*

She also said: *You can't make chicken salad out of chicken shit.*

And certainly this would seem to be supported by everyday evidence. Unhappy millionaires. Happy peasants. Miserable rulers. Cheerful slaves. Literature, in fact, is frequented by such contradictions. Novelists don't tend to write about people who have everything and are happy or people who lack everything and are sad. Books are more interesting when Gatsby pines, or Dilsey endures.

But it is not literature that Dr. Ellis is studying, nor is it even old-fashioned anecdotal life. Dr. Ellis wants hard, empirical proof. And so in addition to compiling his charts, which are largely based on a series of questionnaires and surveys, Dr. Ellis works in the lab. Specifically, he spends a good part of his days with a small army of sad and happy rats.

I ask the obvious question: "How can you tell when a rat is happy?"

He answers my question with a question: "How can you tell when a person is happy?"

I suggest that, for one thing, happy people tend to look happy.

He grins. "And what does that mean?" he asks.

"Well, they smile a lot. They laugh," I say.

Beaming, Dr. Ellis tells me that young rats evince high-pitched chirps when they are tickled or when they engage in rough play with other rats.

"You want to hear them?" he asks eagerly. "It's out of the range of human earshot, but I can hook you up to the speakers—"

"Do I have to tickle them?" I ask.

"You don't want to tickle them?" he says, sounding a bit hurt.

"I'd rather not," I say gently.

Dr. Ellis absorbs this with a confused shrug and leads the way to the lab. Once we are there, his enthusiasm gives way to a gentle, almost patrician benevolence. Taking first one rat, then another from their cages, he strokes them with obvious fondness and seems to probe their flat, ratty eyes for some evidence of cosmic mirth.

"We'll take Harry today," he says, holding on to a gray specimen whom I would not be able to pick out of a rat lineup in a thousand years.

"Harry," Dr. Ellis says, as we walk toward the mazes and receptors, "was just born a happy guy."

I don the listening gear, which is, I'm told, the same gear scientists use to study bats, a species that, for all its navigational instincts, has yet to evince any obvious signs of humor.

Harry waits with what I already perceive as good-natured ease.

At first what I hear is a magnified rustle, the rustle of Harry in his shredded paper. Then Dr. Ellis reaches out and, an impish look on his face, tickles. Harry nips at his fingers, and then there is a high, squeaky sound in the headphones that intensifies.

Happy rats, Dr. Ellis tells me, will persevere in mazes while unhappy rats will not.

Happy rats will eat hearty meals while unhappy rats are finicky.

Happy rats will engage in playful behavior, as well as sexual behavior, more often than unhappy rats.

Happy rats take less time to adjust to changes in sleeping conditions, bunkmates, meals, mealtimes, and all manner of rat-life interruptions.

And unhappy rats sometimes languish after even the mildest obstacles prevent them from achieving their goals.

6

If we only wanted to be happy it would be easy,
but we want to be happier than other people,
which is almost always difficult, since we
think them happier than they are.
—*Montesquieu*

*T.*J.'s sister, Linda, is thirty-nine years old, and no wedding I've ever heard about has been planned with more militaristic precision, or in a spirit of such exquisite revenge. This is to be not just a wedding but a payback for nearly two decades of bridesmaid services rendered.

On the last day of May—Memorial Day weekend, no less—T.J. and I are, consequently, standing in Linda's hotel room, watching in silence as she has her makeup done by a professional makeup artist. She is wearing a sheaf of white satin and an expression of tranquilized charm. She has a towel draped over the top of her dress, and her shoes, although she is wearing them, are wrapped in tissue paper.

"What do you think of the dress?" T.J. asks me.

"Totally princess," I whisper back.

"You don't have to whisper that," T.J. says. "She'd think it was a compliment."

"You're so mean."

"But she's so crazy. Did I tell you she had me go to the candy store at F.A.O. Schwarz to buy her four different shades of green M&M's?"

"Why?"

"So she could pick the right one."

"The right one for what?"

"How the hell do I know?"

I laugh. "Were we ever this crazy?" I ask.

"*I* wasn't," T.J. says. "*You* were pretty intense."

"Go help your sister."

"*You* help her."

"I'm not even supposed to be up here."

"That's true. Where's Michael, anyway?"

I shrug. "Where's Ethan?"

T.J. shrugs.

We share the bemused, wry sigh of modern wives in the act of preferring women's company to men's.

I sit beside Michael during the ceremony, of course, feeling the strong, accustomed grip of his hand, and wondering when it was that I first found his touch to be soothing. There had to have been a moment, I think, when comfort and warmth began to win out over frenzied lust and electric excitement. I know that this must have had something to do with *having* rather than *wanting*, but I find the thought too depressingly trite to contemplate.

Under an enormous chuppah decked with rare vines and spring

flowers, the rabbi offers the wedding vows with a slightly tired air. The tiny glass beads on his dress yarmulke glitter in the video lights.

"Do you promise to love her and honor her, forsaking all others, until death parts you?"

I glance down the row of bridesmaids and see T.J. looking at Ethan, then Ethan looking away.

"Oh, we're fine," T.J. would say. But I see the set of her jaw, and I know that she must be comparing the promise of her sister's marriage to whatever she'll admit to herself is lacking in her own.

I feel Michael squeeze my hand, just as he had during Emily's school play, just as I knew he would during the vows. I squeeze back. I look into his eyes, which, as I've known they would be, are shiny with love. I smile at him. From my childhood until now, I've known these eyes. I have probably looked into them more often than I've looked into my own. And yet it seems almost rare, these days, to be face to face instead of side by side.

Should marriage make you happy? For twenty-five years, married Americans have reported themselves to be happier than unmarried Americans, and in 1991 researchers found a significant relationship between marriage and happiness in sixteen out of seventeen industrialized nations (think twice about living in Northern Ireland). Married people also report fewer psychiatric and medical problems than unmarried people do.

On the other hand, it may be true that it's only the happier people who tend to marry in the first place. According to an article I read in the *Journal of Personality and Social Psychology,* the initial periods before and after a wedding can make almost anyone happier, but the bounce is brief at best. Among 24,000 people studied over the course of fifteen years, the married ones reported themselves only one-tenth of one point happier on an eleven-point happiness scale. Interpreting the results, the director of a Rutgers University think tank on marriage suggested that many marriages fail because of an attempt to sustain an unsustainable glee. Back in the nineteenth century, John Stuart Mill made much the same point. "Most persons," he said, "have but a very moderate capacity of happiness. Expecting . . . in marriage a far greater degree of happiness than they commonly find, and knowing not that the fault is in their own scanty capability of happiness."

"I can't believe it's finally over," T.J. tells me later, when we meet up at the bar.

"You mean all those years of wondering whether she'd ever meet someone?"

"Hell, no. I mean the damned wedding."

"T.J."

"I'm serious. Do you know how many times I've had to hear how happy I must be? Why must I be so happy?"

"Aren't you so happy?"

T.J. grins. "Happiness is a complex emotion," she says, "the mysteries of which will no doubt be brilliantly laid to rest by a soon-to-be-bestselling author."

I force a laugh, pretending that I can be teased about this.

"Every man's happiness," I say, "is built on the unhappiness of another."

"Donald Trump?" T.J. asks me.

"Ivan Turgenev," I say.

It is a predominantly East Side crowd, familiar by look if not by name: young women in sleeveless dresses, sheer stockings, and dangerous shoes. Where and when, I always wonder, were these women taught how to make their tight, shiny ponytails look like a statement of fashion instead of an afterthought? Their bodies are as tidy and straight as their hair, sculpted and refined by hours upon hours of exercise, walking stairs that lead nowhere, riding bikes that go nowhere, rowing phantom rowboats, wearing immovable cross-country skis. The truly rich among them wear large costume pearl or diamond earrings; the less rich wear small real ones. Meanwhile, their husbands make masterful small talk, trying not to do business, scope contacts, or visibly react to the hidden vibrations of cell phones and BlackBerrys in their trouser pockets.

The men are watching the women, of course, but the women are virtually taking notes on and snapshots of one another: shoes, bags, nips, tucks, rings, partners, sizes, hair. Wedding jubilation or not, the room is a kind of teeming agar of envy and fear and rampant insecurity. And the medium that underlies it all is, of course, the search for happiness. Happiness might be Anna's youth. Happiness might be Sylvia's wealth. Happiness might be pregnancy. Fashion. Great hair. Perfect skin. Legs. Money. Fame. Happiness might be having three houses. Having four children. A brilliant career. Happiness might be having three houses, four children, *and* a brilliant career. What's clear to me, at least in this context, is that happiness is invariably what some *other* woman has.

I am staring, despite myself, at the perfectly polished Prada bag that hangs from the perfectly polished shoulder of a school mother named Abbie Prynn. And I wonder: is envy ever the origin of a useful strategy? Or is envy just the illusion that the problem of happiness can be solved?

"Come on. Mingle," T.J. tells me when we meet again at the bar.

"Do I have to?"

"Yes. You have to."

We are crossing the dance floor together when we hear a muffled cry and a crash.

Near the table where the cake plates rise in perfect china towers, an elderly man has clutched his chest, then clutched the tablecloth, then dropped to his knees. This, we find out later, is the groom's uncle, Lysander. Stunned guests look scared, then helpless, then embarrassed that they are helpless. This is not a crowd accustomed to being unsure of what to do.

I look around for Michael but meet, instead, the eyes of a large man with thinning, sandy hair and the most penetrating gaze I have ever seen, a gaze that, impossibly, seems aimed just at me.

"Somebody call someone!" becomes the utterly useless instruction circulating among the crowd, and still this tall man with the sandy hair and the eyes continues to look at me in a way that I find unforgettably calm and eccentric and mysterious. The look is so piercing that it feels like a physical restraint.

I know he can't possibly be looking at me. How can you look with any kind of interest at a total stranger when an old man has just collapsed in a heap by a wedding cake? And yet he continues to look at me, and I continue to stare back at him, and he is so insistent and seems so fascinated that, despite myself, I smile.

When I finally manage to turn away from this look, I see that the old man by the cake table is now gasping. His right hand paws the air. His face is sweaty and bloodless. He looks as if he's in black-and-white, while the rest of the room is in color. I see a mouthful of saliva drop from his lips; I look away. Meanwhile, it is T.J. who races into the kitchen to call an ambulance. And while she does so, I see Michael pushing his way firmly into the chaos.

"He's a doctor," people whisper as Michael comes forward, and they move out of his way.

"That's T.J.'s friend's husband."

"Sally's husband."

"Michael Farber."

The reverent echo of a thousand nights and days.

The large man with the sandy hair has now placed himself by my side, and incongruously, a tiny but confident smile seems to cross his lips as he sees me glance at him. He is neither thin nor fit nor handsome, but to me—though I've turned back to watch the drama—he is suddenly and absurdly the focal point in the room.

Michael, meanwhile, begins his routine, reaching with silent assurance for the old man's wrist, taking his pulse, looking into his eyes.

"I'm Dr. Farber," I hear him say. "Can you talk?"

Wild beyond reason, the old man nods.

"Try to stay calm," Michael says. "Do you have any medical problems? Are you taking any medicines? You're short of breath right now, right?"

"It's hard," the man manages to say.

I feel a hand on my shoulder and nearly jump.

"Is that your husband?" comes the whispered question.

I turn to find a stunning, small, redheaded woman standing beside me.

I nod.

"God, that's right, T.J. told me you were married to a doctor," the woman whispers in what sounds like a mild southern accent. "What a hero. Isn't it awful? I'm Marathon Ross. I've been working with T.J."

One of T.J.'s more prominent coups has been talking the painter Lucas Ross into doing a lush coffee-table book to coincide with the Whitney Museum's upcoming retrospective of his work.

Marathon, I surmise, must be his wife.

"I know all about you," Marathon continues in her whisper. "Gee, you and T.J. go way back. How does she do it? Isn't she amazing? You're so lucky to know her. She's so amazing. This is my husband." And Marathon promptly waves the large man with the eyes into the space between us.

"Lucas Ross," I say to myself wonderingly, then realize I've said it out loud.

"Is that your husband?" he asks me, taking my hand with both his own, which are flat and enormous and cool, and which have painted some of the best-known canvases of the twentieth century.

"Yes," I say stupidly.

"Is he a doctor, or just a very, very good Boy Scout?"

I smile. "Both," I say.

"And what is your name?"

"Sally Farber."

"And what do you do?"

"I avoid writing," I say and force myself to turn back to watch Michael.

The wedding guests begin to come closer, emboldened by the knowledge that their role is now to watch, not help. Sprinting back from the kitchen, T.J. kneels fearlessly next to Michael.

"They're on the way," she tells him.

"Good. Let's get him downstairs. I'll need some help," he says and looks into the frozen crowd.

Two of the waiters lift Uncle Lysander while Marathon scoots forward to hold a door open and gestures impatiently for Lucas to help. I watch as he joins her at the other door and then follows the procession out the ballroom and toward the lobby.

I cannot begin to understand why, but I feel something like true loss when I realize that Lucas has left the room.

7

The greatest happiness of life is the conviction that
we are loved—loved for ourselves, or rather,
loved in spite of ourselves.
—*Victor Hugo*

*T*he last premarital sex of my life was with Jimmy Shannon and took place on top of the cold, gray steel desk at my magazine office. Jimmy, always at his most inspired when sex seemed to be most impossible, had made it his mission to have sex with me on every desk I had ever had. In my days as a budding young magazine editor, that had meant quite a few desktops.

"I read about your promotion," Jimmy would say on the phone in his huskiest voice.

"Yes," I would say.

"You get a new desk with that?" he would ask.

"Come on over and find out," I would say.

And he would come to my office—ostensibly to pitch me new books to excerpt in the magazine—and soon he would lock my door and give me the look that was almost as irresistible as he thought it was.

More often, Jimmy and I used to meet after work at the bookstalls near Central Park. Inevitably I would get there first, no matter how slowly I tried to walk. Inevitably I would tug at my stockings. Test and tame and torture my hair. Check my breath. Pinch my cheeks, because how could I risk the chance of Jimmy seeing me putting on makeup for him?

He would stride across the street, late and eager and traffic-fearless. There was a livid kind of static between Jimmy and me, a crackling flow of stops and false starts. Sex. Affection. Lust. I had never felt such hunger past a first kiss fulfilled. This was, however, insatiable hunger, carbohydrate hunger. This was hunger that burned itself up wanting more.

I was twenty-two years old when I first started seeing Jimmy. I can remember one afternoon when I was wearing sheer white stockings that showed off legs I didn't mind showing; and a peach-colored cotton skirt that buttoned up the front; and a peach and white Hermès scarf tied as a halter top; and maroon leather high heels. Somehow in those high heels I managed to walk halfway across Central Park before I started limping.

"Your shoes?" Jimmy asked then.

"My foot," I lied.

"What's wrong with your foot?" he said.

And because I wanted to torture him, and make him want me, and make myself want him more, I looked down with a coy smile and didn't answer, and he immediately concluded, as I'd intended him to, that this must have something to do with another man, and that if he knew the whole story, it would make him jealous.

He pressed for the whole story.

"Someone you don't want me to know about stepped on your foot?" he asked.

I looked down again, just as coyly.

"You hurt your foot in *bed* with someone else?" he asked, exulting in my treachery.

Five minutes later, under a tree near a then insignificant playground, he was pinning me against the bark, which was lacerating my halter-bare back, and he was kissing me ferociously, and I was not complaining, because pain and pleasure had merged with this man, and it would take an act of magic to separate them again.

The magician was Michael.

Michael and I had stopped being friends when I was twelve and he was fourteen. That was the year his parents split up and he moved out of the building. But first—as he loves to remind me—I insisted that I was never going to talk to him again. It's true I'd decided he was skinny and boring and terminally uncool. He—as I like to remind him—thought I was fast and deep and gorgeous. One day, he had found me in the courtyard with my friend Betsy, drinking Almaden white wine and smoking stale Salems. He had told me that drinking was bad for me. He had told me that cigarettes were bad for me. He had told me that if I didn't promise to stop, he would tell on me. I had told him to mind his own business.

So he moved away without any good-bye, taking his implausible goodness with him. And I stayed behind, forgetting, for a while, that I had once exulted on a night under purple shadows, when he had offered a plastic sapphire as a token of his love.

For a long time, happiness simply seemed to exist on the other side of a carnal equation that began with $x + 1$. The x was always whatever I had, and the $+ 1$ was always the boy, or the man, who was going to make all the difference.

I was sixteen. I was stoned to the point of finding numbers and letters hilarious. Bart Fieldstone had me on his twin bed, with his door locked and his mother down the hall, and perhaps because of the proximity of his mother, he was having a difficult time rolling a condom on and keeping an erection at the same time. So Bart Fieldstone, on this, my very first time, thrust himself at and then into my mouth, but I was wearing braces, and my braces caught on his condom, and I started to laugh, my braces still attached. Laughter did not have the desired effect on Bart and Bart's problem.

When I finally managed to stop laughing and explain to Bart that I was not laughing at him but at the juxtaposition of wire and latex, he shrugged, lighted a new joint, and pulled me back to lie against his tie-dyed pillows.

Sgt. Pepper's Lonely Hearts Club Band was on the record player, and when I heard the words of "With a Little Help from My Friends," I found myself kissing Bart with resolute conviction. I was *going* to lose my virginity. I was *going* to know what the world was always talking and winking about.

"I think you're great," I had the presence of mind to say to Bart, who promptly recovered and revived and tore open a new foil package.

When he came, roughly four hectic minutes later, the Beatles were singing "She's Leaving Home," and I was, mysteriously, weeping, realizing, for the first time, that the other side of the happiness equation could be every bit as familiar as the other side of the world.

After six years of not having seen or heard about each other, Michael and I met again in college, completely by chance. We were eighteen and twenty by then, undergraduates at Brown. By an even greater coincidence, we had signed up for back-to-back hours on the then-exotic terminals in the new computer center.

"Excuse me," Michael said to my back as he came up behind me to take his turn.

"Almost done," I said. I didn't look up. I was watching as the head of the dot-matrix printer zipped back and forth with its rhythmic, high-pitched whine.

"It's three o'clock," Michael said.

"Right."

"Actually, it's a little past three."

"Right. It's just printing out."

"I can see that."

I turned to face him, attempting my most appeasing smile. And then we recognized each other, and he started smiling, and I stopped.

He kissed me after a football game, pretending he had been swept away by the one beer he'd just drunk. We became a couple. We slept nightly on his foldout sofa, beneath an electric blanket with an utterly glamorous dual set of controls. At college, the word *we* was an alien one, but he used it without hesitation. When I was with him, he made me laugh, and I never had to pretend that I was a different kind of person. He understood that I wanted to be a writer and told me he knew that I would be. He loved how I listened to him and loved how I made him feel.

To me, though, the whole thing was too soon and too easy, too blessed by coincidence and fate. It didn't take work, or strategy, or pain. It didn't take being unhappy. Michael was there, knowing what he wanted, all along, and I would fall asleep beside him, hating his loving, generous heart, and the burden it placed on me to decide.

We broke up at least twice during college, and several times after that.

Along the way I dated Ted, who was my one devastatingly drop-dead-handsome-oh-my-God-what's-he-doing-with-me guy. Ted, who would stop his Porsche on the side of the road, lay out enormous lines of cocaine on the top of his dashboard, and challenge me to inhale them all before he started the car and let the wind blow them into priceless clouds of white dust. Talk about happiness. Cocaine happiness! I am brilliant happiness! All my thoughts make sense happiness! All your thoughts make sense! Have a line! Have a cigarette! Life is sweet! I'm *so* happy! I'm so . . . talkative. Wise. Tired. Utterly depressed.

But I digress.

There was sexual happiness too. There was Stuart, whom I met at a colleague's wedding, and who had absolutely nothing to say but once had four orgasms in a night and gave me twice as many.

From time to time, Michael, who was doing his residency at Columbia, would call up and sing me "La Vie en Rose," even though I knew he was fixing catheters and patching up gunshot wounds and learning how to tell people that the people they loved were going to die.

And then, for long stretches of time, there was no one. There were book parties and magazine parties and Christmas parties and me in a proud succession of little black dresses in smaller and smaller sizes that nonetheless left me feeling less and less lovable.

I would go home in a taxi and open the window and close my eyes to feel the nighttime breeze on my face, which would still be flushed from Scotch or from failure. It would be twelve or one in the morning, and I would feel the breeze blowing the tastes and air kisses from me, cleansing me, the streets flying by.

Then this was how I decided that I was going to marry Michael:

We had started dating again, and it was Thanksgiving, and his mother invited us to spend the holiday with her in Vermont.

The last time I had seen Mrs. Farber had been in the elevator of our building. She greeted us with a quavering scream of pleasure, gave us a whirlwind tour of her house, fed us a lavish turkey dinner at noon, and then, when I took out a well-earned cigarette, said she hoped I wouldn't mind, but she didn't allow any smoking in her house.

She was in the vanguard, then, of the antismoking movement. This was in the late eighties, and at the time it was the nonsmokers who seemed a bit eccentric. I politely and obediently put my pack of cigarettes away and looked at Michael for solace, which he gave, but there was nothing that could be done. The short afternoon light was waning, and it was twelve degrees below outside. I couldn't, without being horribly rude, suggest that I wanted to get some fresh air.

Someday, the hidden benefits of nicotine may be discovered. According to an article on the Texas Medical Association website:

> Acute nicotine administration results in increased dopamine release from the CNS, activating the mesolimbic dopaminergic system and producing perceptions of pleasure and happiness, increased energy and motivation, increased alertness, increased feeling of vigor, increased cognitive arousal and increased alertness, similar to that produced by other addictive drugs like heroin or cocaine.

Or, as one of the ads I found for my book put it, more succinctly:

SMOKE NOW!
Be Happy Hereafter

Only heavily addicted smokers can understand how true that statement can seem to be, or can know the sense of emergency that the body creates in the absence of nicotine.

I will say that five hours later, at eight in the evening, I seized the only course that seemed available to me after torture, which was to get into bed and fall asleep in the frigid basement guest room.

It worked for an hour. At nine, I woke up and began to rant. How could anyone not understand that you can't just tell a smoker not to smoke? This was like cutting off someone's oxygen. Couldn't we go to a motel? Couldn't we open a window so I could lean out and just have a few puffs?

With Michael watching me the way that Dr. Ellis would one day watch his rats, I flew from window to window, discovering, to my horror, that Michael's mother had storm windows on every one, storm windows fixed, prisonlike, from outside.

It went on for another hour, until Michael firmly, sweetly, and—again—heroically, took my hand and led me to the tiny bathroom at the foot of the stairs. There, he made me sit next to him on the hideous orange shag carpeting and, despite the fact that he had never taken a puff in his life and had recently completed the pulmonary chapter of his residency, lit a cigarette for me and put it to my lips.

It was brave, it was foolish, it was loving, it was codependent, but there he let me sit. I was planted amid the orange grass of his mother's bathroom's shag carpeting, and I felt totally and irrevocably understood, and for the first time since my childhood, I felt the keen, poignant, irresistible ache of knowing myself to be safe.

I married him wearing a calf-length dress, feeling somehow that at twenty-six I was too old to try to look like a princess. My mother, already resettled in South Carolina—though not yet in her retirement home—made repetitive trips to New York to try to talk me, literally, out of that dress and into something longer.

"You're only a bride once," she said, in a way that made me wonder if she was grandly optimistic or just uniquely unimaginative.

"I don't want to look as if I'm trying to look like some virgin," I told her.

"No one's a *virgin*," she said carelessly. "They still wear *white*. They still wear *gowns*." And she clipped me pictures from *Bride's* magazine, where nobody's ankles were showing.

But I was bent on it being different for me. Perhaps in some way

I hoped I could do something to make this awesome, universal milestone feel like something belonging to me.

I walked down the aisle with my mother in my father's place, and Michael's smile pulling me toward him like the current of a river.

His wedding present to me was a tiny sapphire necklace, the perfect symbol of our past, the perfect symbol of our future.

He would be my protector, my guardian. He would be my partner, my good-luck charm. He would make it seem impossible for anything bad ever to happen to us. And he would love me, even when I wasn't sure he had any reason to love me. Even when I was sure he hadn't.

Of course, to marry Michael seemed to mean that I'd finally found the $+ 1$ after the x and before the equal sign. Or did it only mean that I had changed the value of x?

8

Where fear is, happiness is not.
—*Seneca*

I wake up Monday morning from a dream in which I have fallen, hand on heart, and it is Lucas Ross, not Michael, who is kneeling to offer the comfort and care.

Half embarrassed, half amused, I open my eyes to find that Michael is standing before me, cheerfully toweling off, cheerfully smiling good morning, cheerfully asking if Emily has any clean kneesocks for school. I break our familiar parallel formation to look at him head-on: There are his eyes, with their tiny, fine lashes; his lips, which are always so smooth and dry; his nose, which is large and beaked, a kind of triumph of flesh over space. No doubt if I could strap a listening device to Michael, I would hear emitted a nearly constant high-pitched chirp.

It is a Mardi Gras kind of morning. I get them all out the door at record pace, and the school bus is probably still on our block by the time I am back at my desk upstairs.

I am determined to be back on track. I will not think about strange, dark, piercing famous eyes. I will not set foot in Mom's apartment until I have written at least ten new pages and made at least one trip to the library.

But when the phone rings, I have a bizarre, rogue thought that it is Lucas Ross who's calling, having somehow tracked me down.

Instead, of course, it's my mother—or rather, a proxy of my mother. An eager-sounding woman says her name is Janet McGoogan and informs me that she is my broker.

"You're my broker?"

"Your mother hired me."

"You know my mother?"

"I do now."

"How'd she find you?"

"She called me."

I have a clear image of Mom, her magnifying glass in hand, her nose about a half an inch above the paper as she scans the tiny photos of brokers that the *Times Magazine* always runs in its real estate ads.

"Just a quick look," McGoogan says. "Your mother sounds very motivated."

"Of course she's motivated," I say. "She doesn't have to do the work."

There is an uncomfortable silence, but I choose not to try to dig myself out.

"I'd really love to see it," she says. "How does this afternoon look?"

I manage to put her off, but only for a day.

❋

Several hours later, my panic quotient consequently rising to levels not seen since the week that Emily's birthday party, my book party, and Michael's convention trip coincided, I am sitting in the main-floor lounge of Butler Library at Columbia University, attempting to write a new beginning:

A forty-six-year-old man who has recently quit smoking is walking down a New York street, trailing a woman in mink because she is holding a matchbook in one hand and a cigarette in the other. At the corner, the woman stops, and the man stops behind her. She strikes the match and, because he has aligned his body perfectly with hers, he is able to catch a whiff of the slightly sulfurous smell of her match and the lightly toasted smell of burnt paper. For a moment the man can imagine that he is smoking the cigarette himself, sitting at a desk, or leaning back after a meal, or lying against a pillow. And what he then imagines is that the work he would have just done, or the meal he would have just eaten, or the sex he would have just had, would have been the most sublime and meaningful of his life. In that moment, tied to the spot by thick, smoky ropes, he knows the one thing missing from his life, the one thing he needs to make him happy. He needs a cigarette. If only he could start smoking again, then he would be happy.

At the dawn of the twenty-first century, in the privileged pockets of American life, happiness is an equation that begins not with *If* but *If only*.

Around me are students leaning back to work in upholstered arm-chairs, trusted to drink orange juice and flavored iced coffees while reading borrowed library books and tapping their essays or dreams into laptops.

If only I was their age.

Or is that what I really want? Did I know anything when I was their age? I mean, did I in fact know a single thing?

And how is it possible that they are closer in age to my daughters than they are to me?

Today I am wearing blue jeans, a T-shirt, striped socks, and a pair of running sneakers. My hair is still shoulder length, and mostly brown. But the girl who sold me my cup of coffee called me ma'am not ten minutes ago. And indeed, I have all the telltale signs of ma'am-dom. Road maps of veins have appeared on my legs. Wiry, white hairs spring like question marks from the top of my head. Sleeveless shirts inspire self-doubt. And somehow, when I bend over, I am conscious of a strange sensation of gravity in my face.

What the hell, I think. With any luck, this girl will be ma'amed someday herself.

I continue:

Philosophers, theologians, psychologists, sociologists, biologists, and pharmacologists have all attempted to define happiness. Voltaire and Goethe, Charlie Brown and John Lennon, have chimed in as well. Happiness is stillness. Happiness is goodness. Happiness is a warm puppy. Happiness is a warm gun. The pursuit of happiness has, despite its ever-changing definitions, arguably determined the standards of modern life.

What happiness means is not a new question. Even Aristotle fretted that it would be rare to find two people who might agree on a definition. That, of course, did not deter him from providing his own. Happiness, he wrote in *Nicomachean Ethics,* was "an activity of soul in accordance with perfect virtue." And when he wrote *perfect,* he apparently meant *perfect.* For Aristotle, happiness was not as easy to find as pleasure, nor as hard to come by as fortune or luck. In his view, every human being was meant to find his greatest calling in the service of and love for other human beings. The notion that happiness could be achieved without moral goodness but with, say, a prescription drug pad, would have left him totally cold.

I look up from my writing and count the black tiles in the linoleum floor and listen to the clink of the bottles that the girl is now loading into the vending machine.

Shafts of spring sunlight enter and exit the room like ghosts.

Two brown-haired students—they have to be freshmen, they look so incredibly young—bend their heads together, laughing, glancing sideways at a male student, then nuzzling back down into their books. I think of Katie and Emily, so close to their first departure, and then to the lightning storm of departures that will follow, and then they'll each be sitting in a library lounge somewhere, giggling, studying, being whoever it is they are going to be. I feel a cramp of pride and terror at the thought, and then somehow the afternoon disappears into a cottony paralysis. I wander the stacks, looking for books and then forgetting the titles, and having to look them up again, and I reread my new paragraphs, trying to will myself into writing more, as if the momentum can trick me forward. And so on Tuesday, while I should be writing again, I am instead escaping to Mom's apartment, bearing a bouquet of cleaning supplies and a bucket as a vase.

Janet McGoogan's inspection is thorough, her conclusion unforgiving.

"You can rent it or sell it in this state and hope for the best. Or you can invest a little to fix it up and the payoff will be enormous. With some fairly simple improvements in décor and paint, we could be talking about a difference in sales price of a hundred thousand dollars."

I can almost hear the pleas from my mother, wafting north on a mendicant breeze.

"I've got the perfect decorator for you!" T.J. says on the phone the next morning.

I am trying to have our morning talk and to dress for my meeting with Jimmy at the same time.

"No way," I tell her. "You know I can't afford your guy."

"I'm not talking about André," she says. "You can't afford André."

"That's what I just said," I tell her. Does she know when she's rubbing it in?

"I'm talking about Lucas Ross's wife. I've told you about her. Marathon. Wait. She said she met you at the wedding."

"Thanks anyway," I tell her.

"I'm really serious, Sally," T.J. says. "She's got a great sense of design. She's been incredibly helpful on his book. She's done their Amagansett house and their apartment, and they're both amazing. And I know she really wants to start her own business. Why don't you meet her at least?"

I tell T.J. I'll think about it, but jobbing this out does not hold much appeal. My mother's apartment is mine: to have, to hold, to wreck, and to repair.

There are too many reflective surfaces between the Times Square subway stop and Jimmy's office. Actual mirrors, black glass windows, polished metal doors. In every one I pass, I rediscover not only how startlingly old my face has become but also how quickly the smile I affix to it fades from mirror to mirror.

One of the researchers I've interviewed, citing a recent study of some particularly happy Tibetan monks, claims that even a forced smile can engender happiness, and make other people smile as well.

I force a smile. The man I next pass on the street, however, offers me not a smile in return but what looks like a grimace of shock and concern.

In the elevator, where real mirrors panel the walls, part of me is hoping to see the woman I was when I used to wear suits. I look instead at my shoes—the least scuffed of my rubber-soled flats— and marvel at the thought that I ever wore high heels to work every day. Yet somewhere, I feel certain, a Tibetan monk is smiling.

Jimmy's greeting is, predictably, a French Foreign Legion double-cheeked kiss.

"So," he says, settling in behind his desk and looking into my eyes with the look that used to slay me.

"Maybe people just don't like to read about nice things," I say. I am referring—and he knows it—to the near-historic disaster of *The History of Love.*

"I think people just don't like to get serious about love," Jimmy says. "Goodness knows I don't."

"Are you going to cancel the contract?" I ask.

"What?"

"For *Happiness.* Are you going to take the advance back?"

He frowns at me. "What's wrong, Cookie?"

"You must have taken a bath on the last one," I say.

"Well?"

"Well, aren't you worried?"

"Are you going to give me some pages to read?"

"How's the Lama doing this week?" I ask.

"Running out of steam," Jimmy says.

He pushes his chair back and puts his feet up on the desk. He has gained some weight in the last few years, but there is still something quick and boyish about him.

"Well, what have you learned about happiness?" he says and reaches for his pack of cigarettes.

"Happiness," I say, accepting the fact that at this moment I would be perfectly content to define happiness as a cigarette and a desk to smoke it at. I smile. "Happiness," I say, "is a cigarette and a desk to smoke it at."

He grins and offers the pack to me, but I shake my head.

"Keep talking," he says.

"Some people think there's a gene for it," I say. "A happiness set point. Like in weight. Some people think it's friendship. Aristotle thought it was virtue. No one has a different definition of anger, or sadness, or envy. But happiness is—it's—a shimmer. It's a note. Trying to describe it is like trying to describe music. Or color. Or taste. It's reaching your toes down and finding the cool part of the sheets. It's hearing the song you were trying to remember. It's fresh cheesecake and a cup of coffee. Breast-feeding. Victory. Hope. It's knowing exactly what you're supposed to do. Love. Being loved. *Falling* in love. Making things. Feeling safe. Knowing exactly what you're supposed to do—"

"You said that already."

"Oh, Jimmy," I say. Horrifyingly, my eyes fill with tears.

"You didn't have this much trouble with the other books," he says, oblivious to or perhaps simply resistant to my tears.

"I understood the others better," I say.

"Anger?" he says.

"Yes."

"Jealousy? Love?" he says.

"Yes," I say. I lower my head.

"What other emotions do you understand?" Jimmy asks.

"I understand fear," I say.

9

❊

Before we set our hearts too much upon anything,
let us examine how happy they are,
who already possess it.
—*François de La Rochefoucauld*

*L*ucas Ross became famous in the early 1970s when his painting *SILLY* was purchased by the Museum of Modern Art. It was
an iconic eight-foot-by-eight-foot canvas, layered in the irresistible
shades and shadows of blue and black that would become his trademark. In the center of the canvas was the word *SILLY*, painted in
tiny white letters, and above it—like a pair of mirthful eyes—were
two dabs of white paint.

People argued over this painting the way they had argued over
Pollock's drips and Rothko's color blocks and Stella's stripes and
Warhol's soup cans, and the argument made news, in an art-

community kind of way. Dozens of articles were predictably titled "What Is Silly?" and pondered the question of Ross's intent: to mock modern art, or artists, or to inspire emotions and talk. Critics debated the meaning of the two white dots and wondered if at least some of the blue and black shapes were meant to be figurative.

But what drew the most attention was Lucas Ross's reaction to the attention. Who else but Lucas Ross would have shown up for a gallery opening wearing black pants and a turtleneck that he had painted with the word *SILLY* and two dabs of paint on his chest?

SILLY, from that moment on, became an icon of the seventies, much as Robert Indiana's *LOVE* had been an icon of the sixties. And Lucas Ross became *Ross* that year, the way that Rauschenberg would be *Rauschenberg,* and Hockney would be *Hockney.*

He was, however, just beginning. *SILLY* was soon joined by:

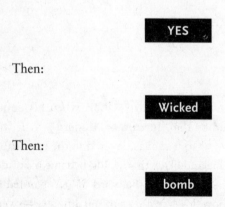

YES

Then:

Wicked

Then:

bomb

Next Ross traded words for phrases, beginning a new series with lines taken from TV and movies.

Here's Johnny

And:

> I'd rather kiss a wookie

And:

> WE'RE GOING TO NEED A
> BIGGER
> BOAT

His paintings became T-shirts; T-shirts became his paintings. And then, just as parodies were becoming rife, he began a period of almost completely figurative work, proving to everyone not only that he could paint without gimmick or irony but that he could paint as beautifully, as movingly, as sincerely, and as originally as any master had.

I ponder all this on Thursday, when, back at work with most of June and the subject of happiness in art before me, I sit with a pile of picture books in the humid stacks of Butler Library. My ostensible purpose is to gather examples of visual art that deal with the theme of happiness, but when I come upon Lucas Ross's work, I find myself stopping to read, and to look. The large, glossy pages feel cool beneath my hands. I turn another page and find another portrait. A woman, seated, holding a blue flower.

I wonder if this is Marathon, the wife I met at the wedding, or whether Lucas was married before her, or whether he usually works with a model, and incidentally, whether if I had a name like *Marathon* I would instantly be a size four. The canvas is titled *Waiting for Spring* and was painted in 1987. "Collection of Lucas and Marathon Ross," I read. Would they still own the canvas if the woman was a former wife? The woman's expression, in the painting, is shy and tired and hopeful. I rest my cheek on the page for a minute, feeling its comforting coolness.

Visions of happiness show up with startling frequency in the history of art.

Unlike literature, in which conflict is essential to storytelling and thus to success, visual art can portray joy, serenity, comfort, glee, pleasure—even contentment—without fear of provoking boredom.

The halls of museums certainly teem with brilliant scenes of battles and biblical crises, with portraits of people in pain, in confusion, or in poverty. But the portrait of the Mona Lisa is, apart from anything else, a study of happiness. And da Vinci was hardly alone in his willingness to take on the subject. Rembrandt's burghers were contented. Edward Hicks's kingdoms were peaceable. Even the ox seemed to be smiling.

Matisse and Cassatt, Copley and Klee all made their own visual odes to joy. Renoir's couples twirled, and Chagall's lovers flew through space. All would have been disastrous subjects for plays or novels. All made for great paintings. And what I learn in the stacks of Butler Library is that when Lucas Ross gave up the irony of his word paintings for the mastery of form, he seemed as much to be describing happiness as he had been, previously, merely trying to provoke it.

No, I think. It is not really hope that I see on the face of the woman in the portrait. It is something closer to longing, but also a kind of joy.

Perhaps it is true that, as Bertrand Russell once suggested, "To be without some of the things you want is an indispensable part of happiness." I think of this as the Rhonda Popkin Theorem, because the first thing in my life that I ever desperately wanted and couldn't have was the friendship of Rhonda Popkin, the most popular girl in my kindergarten class. Rhonda Popkin had a Dutchboy haircut and a slightly porcine nose and not very good breath, but with a genius for fickle devotions, she also had the ability to send several dozen five-year-old girls into a frenzy of desire. On the very first day of school, Rhonda declared that I was going to be her best friend, and then, for the next thirty weeks or so, she did not say a word to me.

And the kindergarten world—filled though it eventually became with pumpkin carvings and Christmas cookies and Easter egg hunts—also became a world filled with pain. Rhonda Popkin held the key to my happiness, and she didn't let it go.

Not until I was in my late twenties did I realize that if it hadn't been Rhonda Popkin, it would have been someone else. Inevitably, and for whatever reasons, fair or unfair, someone would have rejected me, and from the seed of that rejection would grow the scary, gorgeous, overly fragrant bloom of longing. This flower would become my adornment and would dictate my other adornments; like all other people, I would be shaped just as much by what I had as by what I'd been made to want. And in the strange, backward way of life's important things, desire would become as much a part of happiness as happiness was a part of desire.

"I just talked to Janet McGoogan," Mom tells me on the phone that night.

"Uh-huh," I say, with the phone tucked under my ear and all the recognizable vegetables I could find in the fridge laid out before me to chop for a stir-fry.

"What have you done to the place?" Mom asks.

"Excuse me?"

"What have you done to the place? Janet says it's a total mess."

"Mom, *I* told you it was a total mess."

"You didn't tell me you were pulling up kitchen tiles."

I pause, catching my breath, but am overruled by a primal instinct.

"I wasn't," I say.

It is probably the first time that I've told a direct lie to my mother in twenty years. What the hell is wrong with me?

"How did the tiles get that way, then?" she says, doing her part of the scene with perfect pitch. "Do you think they just walked into a pile all by themselves?"

"I wanted to see what was underneath."

"You knew what was underneath," she says.

"I wanted to see it anyway."

"I can't imagine why."

Amazing. It's our entire relationship, reduced to four simple statements.

"She doesn't understand me," I say to Michael that night.

He looks at me appraisingly, and for a moment I think that he's angry, or at least that he's impatient. But he has just cursed out the Yankees, so he's more inclined to be tolerant with me.

"She has never understood you," he says. "She will never understand you. Conjugate this with me. She hasn't. She doesn't. She can't. She won't."

"What makes you so wise?" I ask him.

He polishes off the last of his cereal.

"Wise?" He stands up and stretches. "If I'm so wise, why can't I understand the mind of George Steinbrenner?" Disgustedly, he flicks the TV off and tosses the clicker to the foot of the bed.

"How was your day?" I ask him.

"Just fine," he says, either too tired to offer details or aware that I'm too tired to absorb them.

So we march on into the evening, side by side and shoulder to shoulder. We have our jokes, our rules, our assigned tasks, our war stories, our scars, our medals. Maybe in marriage you just can't remain face-to-face if you want to get anything done: if you want to watch out for your children, say, or write, or read, or doctor, or cook, or occasionally have clean clothes to wear.

❋

On Monday, I go back to Mom's apartment, where—with less than three weeks to go before the girls leave for camp—the solitude feels considerably more like a choice and less like a threat.

As I walk in, though, I confront the archaeological dig site that is the kitchen floor. Resolutely, I begin to fill trash bags with the detritus of the dig. It is a little depressing, what I've wrought, especially because there are a few tiles in the center of the room that seem to have been fixed by some kind of supernatural adhesive force and that, despite my best efforts the previous week, could not be chipped apart from the old tiles beneath them. The effect is that of a beat-up blue floor on which someone has dropped some ragged wood chips—and the resulting *Candid Camera*–ripe impulse is to bend over and pick them up.

I lack the energy to solve this problem, so I go instead to the living room and open yet another of the doctor's file cabinets and am surprised and delighted to find real files, separated by hand-labeled dividers:

Absolutism
Africa
Aggression
Aging

The doorbell rings.

Capitalism
Cathedral
Catholicism

The doorbell rings again.

A file folder still in my hand, I open the door expecting to see the handyman, and find instead an annoyed-looking T.J.

"Why didn't you answer the door?" she asks.

"What are you doing here?" I counter.

"God, it really is a pit," she says in a way that makes me want to defend the apartment against her standards.

T.J. steps in and looks distastefully at the foyer, with its pock-marked salmon walls.

"What are you doing here?" I ask her again. "Is everything okay?"

"Yeah," T.J. says. "I don't know," she adds, forging past me into the doctor's office.

She points to the open filing cabinets. "Anything interesting in there?" she asks.

"I really don't know yet," I say and swiftly toss the folder I'm holding into the nearest drawer.

"Anything, for example, about the history of happiness?"

"Don't tell me. Jimmy sent you," I say.

T.J. sits down in the cracked leather desk chair. "No, of course not," she says wearily. She takes off her jacket. "It's fucking roasting in here," she says.

"T.J. What is the problem?" I ask.

"I don't know. I just wanted to get away. I just thought—"

For the first time, I notice that she is carrying her briefcase.

"What's in there? A manuscript?" I ask.

T.J. grins and smiles with unconcealed pride.

"It's Tom Wolfe's," she says.

"No way."

She strikes a Rocky-style pose, then does a victory dance.

"How'd you get it?"

"Charm!" she cries. "And you wouldn't believe the screaming from FSG! They're furious!"

(Maybe happiness is just sticking it to Tom Wolfe's last publisher.)

"And you want to read it here?"

"Could I? It's just a zoo at the office. The phone keeps ringing. You know how it is."

For an hour or so, she reads in silence, clearly riveted. I wonder if Tom Wolfe is happy. I wonder if Tom Wolfe has ever had a day of writer's block in his life.

Suddenly, T.J. looks up. "You think it's Ethan, don't you?" she asks, and I realize that I have paused in my file sorting to stare at her.

"What?"

"You think I'm freaking out about Ethan, right?"

She is poised for an answer, having stretched out elegantly, without irony, on what was once the therapist's treatment couch.

"It's not Ethan," she says, answering her own question.

"I didn't say anything," I say.

T.J. looks back down at the manuscript and turns another page.

"Did he fall asleep last night, or could he not—" I start.

"He could not," T.J. says, without looking up.

"Have you thought about seeing a sex therapist?"

"Oh, right, like he'd really do that."

"Or a marriage counselor?"

"Our marriage is fine," she says, finally looking at me. "It's just our sex life that isn't."

I stare back at her a moment, wondering if she is making a joke but realizing almost immediately that she is completely serious.

"What?" she says, seeing the look on my face, which I'm not quick enough to conceal.

"Nothing," I say.

"Something funny?"

"Nothing. So what are you going to do?"

"Well, I thought I'd finish this manuscript."

"About Ethan, I mean."

"I don't know. Stop talking about it," she says.

"No problem."

"The Prynns are getting a divorce," she says, as if that is changing the subject.

"Really," I say. "Who told you?"

"Abbie," she says. "I ran into her at Saks."

"How was she?"

"She said she should have done it years ago."

"How are the kids?"

"I didn't ask," she says.

"Wow," I say.

"He was a real shit to her, though," T.J. says. "You know, he was screwing around all over the place." She says this with barely concealed enthusiasm. Better, I guess, to have a sexually dysfunctional but loyal spouse than a cheater with working parts.

And is there a difference, I wonder, watching the ease with which T.J. settles back into her reading, between the happiness of being happy and the happiness of being happy because you think someone might be less happy than you?

I return to the doctor's quaint alphabetical subject dividers—

Darwin
Dementia
Depression
Dolor

And of course I am desperate to see what's under "Happiness," but I find that the doctor had skipped the subject entirely, going in her capricious way from "Greed" to "Greek" to "Grief" to "Hope."

"Do you guys have sex like every night?" T.J. asks me.

"What?" I say, closing the file cabinet.

"Do you?" T.J. asks again. "Do you have sex every night?"

"Oh, come on," I say.

"But look, you probably do sometimes think of yourself as sexy, don't you?"

Into my mind, like a too-bright light, flashes the unexpected memory of Lucas Ross's eyes.

"Yes," I say to T.J. "I sometimes think of myself as sexy."

10

Seek not happiness too greedily,
and be not fearful of happiness.
—*Lao-tzu*

*I*n the second and third weeks of June, the girls, freed at last from school, trudge off to the park with Frieda and go to friends' houses for playdates and, when I'm with them, push every button I have. Rationally, I know that they must be nervous about leaving, but knowing this does not make them even a little bit less annoying.

Incompetence has descended upon them like a fine mist. Suddenly, they are unable to turn on the shower, find their running shoes, keep a civil tone of voice. They pout, they stalk, they roll their eyes, they strap their hands, like six-shooters, to their hips. I am stretched tight between the two maternal poles: the dread of the empty, silent nest and the urge to find a large mallet and bludgeon the chicks.

On Wednesday, heading over to Mom's, I pass four large sidewalk squares of newly poured concrete. The squares have been roped off to keep them pristine while they're drying, but clearly at least one pigeon didn't get the memo, because there are eight or ten bird footprints tracing a nervous arc along the top of one square. I can't help feeling awful that somewhere in this city there is a pigeon whose toes are growing heavier and heavier as the concrete on them dries. What a shock to the system to realize that what you've stepped in can't be washed away.

That's no way to leave a nest, either, I think, and a cartoon image pops into my mind of a pigeon flapping madly to keep aloft, despite the tiny concrete blocks that are drying around its toes.

At Mom's apartment, I spend a solid hour peacefully scrubbing the bathroom floor. The grime comes off the tiles in layers, lightening the white and deepening the black. I work in sections, twenty tiles by twenty tiles, relishing the contrast between the before and after. Maybe, I think, happiness is simply order. In Kurt Vonnegut's novel *Cat's Cradle,* I remember, one character's reaction to the apparent destruction of the world was to pick up a broom and start sweeping. Of course that was a response to the destruction of the world, and all I'm faced with is the temporary disruption of one tiny, otherwise intact family unit. Just eight weeks, I tell myself. Just eight weeks.

Because somehow, in the stillness and silence of this tiny black-and-white tiled room, with the intoxicating perfume of Mr. Clean and the certainty of knowing when something is finished and when it's not, somehow, it becomes clear to me that this moment, this mood, this eccentric summer is all about my girls.

Because this is what they don't tell you about motherhood:

They don't tell you that you have to fall madly, deeply, irrevocably in love, so that your whole life is changed, your whole rhythm altered, your whole heart opened—and then, just when you've reached the point when you think you can tell exactly what kind of day they've had by the way their braids are hanging, you have to pretend that the prospect of them sleeping two hundred miles away from you is absolutely no different from the prospect of them sleeping four yards away.

They don't tell you that you have to stroke and caress and feed and hold and brush and clip and trim and soothe, and then, with the very same hand, you have to wave a convincingly cheerful good-bye.

They don't tell you that you have to be both the spectator cheering madly and the actor who knows how the show always ends.

The following Wednesday, Frieda has a bad tooth, and so, somewhat reluctantly, I bring the girls to Mom's apartment. I am not entirely thrilled about sharing my new cool hangout, but I bring along watercolors and paper because my mother's birthday is coming up, and handmade presents will be expected. And while I Frisbee cracked china and glassware into a large garbage can, the girls sit at the kitchen table and take out the paints.

Eventually, meaning only to stop for a drink of water, I sit beside them and take out a piece of watercolor paper and a thick brush with a red handle and white bristles. I dip the brush into the water and then into the paint, and I make a line, which at the second it bleeds into the paper becomes, magically, the horizon of a seascape.

"Do you like mine, Mommy?" Katie asks.

"Wonderful," I say, sincerely admiring the freedom of her abstract brushstrokes. She will do four paintings in the time it will take Emily and me to do half of one. Beside her at the table, Emily shields her paper with her arm, as if she is taking a final exam. For the moment I am spared the challenge of having to like-hers-too-but-differently. Lazily, the three of us paint for a while in silence.

"Almost done," Emily says now, as much to herself as to us, I know. I envy—and dimly recognize—how thorough and private her concentration is when she is making things.

"What are you painting, Mom?" Katie asks me.

"The three of us," I say. "In a boat," I add, in case that isn't clear.

"Why is it so dark?" Emily asks, and I look down at my paper to discover that I have covered every last inch of it with the shadowy, unmistakably Rossian colors of blue and black.

Michael and I decreed long ago that Saturday night would be Date Night. Through the early days of parenthood, through the perils of nursing, separation anxiety, and potty training, through the monsters in the closet and the bullies in the playground, we have remained determined to keep at least one patch of time for ourselves.

We have, as a consequence, gotten tired—sometimes to the point of vertigo—in an impressive variety of Manhattan's cultural venues. We have stifled yawns at jazz concerts, the Temple of Dendur, and too many movies to name. We have left after the first act of probably half a dozen Broadway plays and then sought a cab only halfheartedly, biding our time until we knew that the girls would be safely tucked in bed.

In fact, we don't usually want to go out as much as we want to stay in. What we really want, what in fact we crave, is to cuddle in bed with the phone turned off and a stack of magazines to read and an old movie in the VCR and dinner on trays and sex afterward, maybe even more than once.

We long to be supine, without the girls' voices—and sometimes the girls themselves—forever shooting into our bedroom like bright, sharp arrows. Occasionally, Michael even insists that we try it. He unplugs the phone and orders the girls a pizza and asks Frieda to keep them at bay. But inevitably, something happens that seems to require intervention or rescue.

❋

Tonight, we are supposed to be dining with T.J. and Ethan. Despite the frequency of my contact with T.J., we rarely meet with our husbands along. Michael and Ethan have in common neither sensibility nor experience. Every once in a while—hope springs eternal—T.J. and I set up a dinner, but tonight Michael is even less anxious than usual to keep the date.

"I don't see why you had to schedule something for tonight," he says.

"Because you usually like doing things on Saturday nights," I say, looking into the mirror and applying my lipstick as if it is a smile.

"It's our last weekend with the girls before they go," he says.

"T.J. knew we were free. What was I going to say?"

"You could have said that we wanted to spend our last weekend with the girls."

Why don't I want to be home tonight too? I'm not entirely sure, but it seems the same impulse that has catapulted me into a one-woman wrecking crew at my mother's apartment now has me brushing my hair up into a bun, putting on a silk blouse, and wanting to run like hell from the people with the woodland-creature eyes who at this moment are circling our bedroom, their sadness too much a reproach, their sweetness too much a temptation.

We go to a T.J.-chosen place on the Upper East Side, where she seems to know half the people in the front room alone, and then we sit, couple to couple, with males and females forming diagonal lines, crossing like swords.

Most of the talk is about the children. School troubles, junk food, tactics for bedtime. The postmortem on the school play. The amount and types of candy we're planning to sneak into the camp trunks. We usually avoid all talk of work, because Ethan doesn't have enough of it and Michael has too much. But tonight, Ethan is brimming with new-idea confidence.

"I've got it," he says.

"What have you got?" T.J. asks him briskly, trying to conceal her dread.

"Okay. It's a Hunch."

"What's a hunch?"

"Remember Pet Rocks?" Ethan asks.

"Pet what?"

"A rock that came in a box that said 'Pet Rock' on it."

"I remember them," Michael says.

"Okay. So I sell Hunches. People would say, 'Do you have a Hunch?' And 'This is my Hunch.' Or Scruples. What about Scruples?"

"Like, 'The perfect gift for the woman with no Scruples,' " I say.

"Exactly! I've got a whole list here," Ethan says, unfolding a printed page.

"I could sell a Lurch. A Huff. A Tizzy," Ethan goes on. "Qualms. Doubts. Nuances. Trifles."

"Peeves," Michael adds.

"What?"

"Pet Peeves."

"Maybe."

"Just one thing," T.J. says. "What do they look like?"

"What?"

"Hunches. Qualms. Peeves."

"I haven't worked that part out yet."

"Oh."

"Except for the Qualm."

"You feel you know what the Qualm looks like."

"Yes. It looks something like a mole."

❄

No one is disappointed when the waiter brings the check. But on our way out, we are blocked by a crowd of patrons who have formed a semicircle around a small table and, seemingly transfixed by the scene before them, are robotically raising torpedo-shaped flutes of champagne. T.J. and I have to stand on tiptoe to see what's going on.

Then we recognize the players. A beaming Lucas Ross is hefting a preposterously large diamond ring onto his wife's right hand, apparently announcing his engagement to her. Marathon's cheeks are pink as salmon, though whether in embarrassment or passion it is impossible to tell.

"I don't believe this," T.J. says.

"Why is he doing this?" I whisper to her.

"Let's get out of here before they see me," T.J. hisses.

But it's too late. Marathon gives a royal wrist-twist wave, and Lucas catches my eye and at the same time exuberantly announces: "The most beautiful, wonderful, magical woman in the world is going to marry me!"

Patrons scramble to find surfaces on which to put their glasses so that they can applaud this momentous announcement. Lucas, tall and shaggy and so alive, embraces Marathon, leading with his pelvis, and kisses her searchingly. T.J., meanwhile, looks as if she has just run over a small animal—perhaps, I think, a Qualm.

With Lucas expansively leading the way, and merrily greasing the maître d' in passing, T.J. and Ethan and Michael and I return to the table that we've just left.

Marathon brings up the rear and then melts into one of the extra chairs that the waiter has brought over.

Marathon is indeed a stunningly, almost disturbingly beautiful woman. Whatever color her hair originally was, it is now a fairly convincing coppery red, and it is thick and perfectly blown dry. She has pale, perfect skin that looks as if it has been stretched as an artist's canvas; where her cheeks meet her ears, there are small eddies of pale, soft hairs, like the down on a baby's neck. The softness of that skin and down make the ideal contrast to her eyes, which are lucidly green, and seem to melt and blaze at exactly the same time.

Three elderly women come over to her.

"I just wanted to tell you what a beautiful thing that was."

"Best wishes, dear."

"So romantic."

And then, like warbling birds, they descend on Lucas.

"What a charming way to propose."

"Whatever gave you the idea?"

"If only my husband—"

Lucas shakes each of their hands, looks into each set of sharp, bright eyes, showers them with gratitude, so that by the end of their five minutes at his side, they probably feel that they have been intimately involved in the launching of a new marriage. I notice that Marathon, while flashing the glittering new ring on her right hand, has been sportingly keeping her left hand in her lap. But when one of the women leans down to say good-bye, and almost knocks a champagne glass over, Marathon reaches up to grab it, and the woman sees her wedding ring.

"But—" the woman begins.

"You see—" Lucas starts.

"I'm already married," Marathon says, in her soft southern way.

"But—" the old woman says again.

"To me," Lucas says. "She's married to me."

The women bob their heads slightly and nervously, as if they are pecking the air.

"He does this," Marathon says, as if by way of explanation.

"You mean . . . even *though* you're married?"

"That's right," Lucas says proudly. "I want her to know I'd still want her to marry me. Even if we'd just met."

"But that's wonderful!" one of them says and sets off a new round of congratulations.

Lucas, absorbing their attention like sunlight, seems unaware that Marathon, the object of his affection, has just, after politely requesting and receiving permission, downed the remainder of both T.J.'s and my champagne glasses, and exuberantly signaled the waiter for another one of her own.

Meanwhile, I feel suddenly conscious of every single component of my appearance. I rearrange my hair, roll up the sleeves I've just rolled down, reapply my lipstick, and note, for the first time this evening, that one of my fingernails has blue paint beneath it.

Lucas is filled with brio, and I cannot stop looking at him, and when the old women have finally twittered away, and Lucas has turned back to the table, tall with praise, and satisfied, I feel myself brighten inside his smile. I was half asleep fifteen minutes ago, but now I would gladly barhop all night.

He has his arm draped around Marathon's shoulder, and he is talking about his latest work.

"It's the hours that have been getting to me these days," he is saying. He fingers his champagne glass with his huge, astonishing hands.

"The hours?" Michael asks.

"Yes. Killing hours. Well, finishing this book for *this* lady," Lucas says, gesturing to T.J. "And getting ready for the show at the Whitney. We're not even going out to the Island this summer."

"Well, neither are we, if that's any consolation to you," T.J. says.

"Well, neither are we," I put in. "But then, we never have."

They laugh.

"There seems to be less and less time these days," Lucas adds.

"Just more obligations," Michael says pleasantly.

"What do you do?" Lucas asks Michael.

"I'm a doctor," Michael says.

Marathon says to him: "Lucas. The wedding. Remember? That poor man with the heart attack?"

"Ah, yes, of course," Lucas says. "I guess it would be stretching the point to say that you try to save lives and I try to save spirits?" he asks Michael.

Michael smiles politely. The rest of us laugh, and Ethan says: "Sometimes, I try to save money," and we laugh again.

"Sally tries to save paper," T.J. says. "That's why she hasn't finished her book yet."

"Busted," I say. And then I feel a hand on my knee and, at exactly the moment that I realize it cannot possibly be Michael's, I look across the table and see the same dark, impossible, dangerous look on Lucas's face that I saw at the wedding. And though I reach down intending to remove his hand with my hand, I end up, instead, allowing it to engulf mine.

Naturally, after dinner, I decide to seduce Michael.

I take him to Mom's apartment, undoing, in my mind, the clutch of hand on hand.

Ostensibly, we are here just so that Michael can finally see the place. But when we enter the doctor's office, with its view of the moonlit reservoir and its aura of ancient secrets, I turn to kiss Michael, hard.

"Do you realize when we were teenagers how many times I fantasized about having sex with you in this place?" he asks.

I kiss him hard again.

"This is good," Michael says.

"Mmm," I say.

"Here?" he says.

"Mmm," I say again.

"We don't have to lock the bedroom door," he says.

"I know."

"Or not shout out."

"I know."

"We could do it right here," he says.

He pulls me down to the rug and lies beside me and kisses my shoulder, then my arm. I close my eyes. It is the easiest way I know of to see myself the way I want to be. He kisses my breasts. He kisses the place between them.

He is wearing his boxer shorts. Then he is reaching down to remove them. Then he is hard, sweeping against my thigh, then flattened against my belly, pressing. I strain to kiss him, eyes still closed, landing my mouth on his neck by mistake, then opening my eyes to find his shoulder, which I kiss, too, trying to mask my lack of direction. Michael does not seem to notice, or mind. Inside me now. No kisses left. I close my eyes again, hugging him with my legs, lifting him with my thighs.

Lucas would not accept closed eyes, I think. Lucas would need to be watched, applauded, attended through any voyage, whether sexual or not. Closed eyes to Lucas would not signify depth or passion.

They would signify distance, autonomy, and he would consider those a rebuke. His eyes would need to be open, open, and I would have to have mine open, I would be open. I open my eyes. For a moment, the eyes I meet have the dark focus of Lucas's, and then, with the change of the light, they become the mild, warm brown of Michael's, and he comes, sighing, and I keep my eyes open, which is the only way I know not to see what I don't want to see.

11

✳

To be stupid, selfish, and have good health are
three requirements for happiness, though if
stupidity is lacking, all is lost.
—*Gustave Flaubert*

*T.*J. shows up at Mom's apartment again on Monday afternoon, a
bottle of Chablis in her hand and murderous envy in her eye.

"Susannah Estes is being promoted," she says.

"Who is Susannah Estes?"

"You know. That bimbo who started in accounting."

"I thought she was at Simon and Schuster," I say.

"She is."

"So what does that have to do with you?"

She gives me the same look that Katie and Emily give me when
I tell them it doesn't matter who got the bigger pancake. Then she
makes a beeline for the kitchen, where she slams the cabinet doors,

looking for a wineglass, and settles instead for a blue-tinged high-ball, one of the few items that survived my recent cabinet purge.

She washes the glass. She pours. She drinks.

"Is it really so bad?" I ask her.

She fixes me with a lethal stare.

"Is it really so bad that your kids are going to camp?" she asks.

"That was a low blow," I say, and she laughs.

"*I'm* counting the days till mine are out of here," she says.

"Fine, but you've still got a baby at home. Just wait," I say.

"I *can't* wait," she says. "The thought of having all that peace and quiet—"

But T.J. does not want peace and quiet any more than a carp wants air. Even now, she has multiplied the chaos around her: there are papers of hers on the doctor's desk, on the doctor's couch. There is a sense of pressure around her, a sense that things could always blow. Even when she is sitting still, you know she is working on something. You can tell, the way you can tell a pot with a flame beneath it from a pot that doesn't have one.

"I've got too much going on," T.J. says.

"You always have too much going on," I say.

"I know. But now—I don't know."

"Paxil. Zoloft. Wellbutrin," I say.

"Moe. Larry. Curly," she says.

I look at her.

"I do not suffer from depression," T.J. says.

"I know that."

"I'm just—I don't know—depressed."

"You think there's a distinction there?"

T.J. looks at me, instantly furious. "There's a *huge* distinction!" she almost shouts. "Depression is like, just, some *clinical* thing or something, like an illness. *Feeling* depressed is different. It's just—you know, I have a lot of depressing things in my life! *Anyone* would be depressed!"

And her marriage is great, it's just her sex life that's the problem.

And her kids are fine.

And her job is fine.

And she's making perfect sense, right?

I understand what she's trying to say, of course: being depressed *about* something is not exactly the same as being depressed. But she's splitting a nearly invisible hair. Because the truth is that there are thousands of women who, in her life, would be thrilled, and the fact that she is not thrilled *does* say something about her (just as the fact that I am pulling up kitchen floors when I should be writing a book says something about me), and the something it says is not necessarily an indictment of her entire value as a human being. But it does mean something.

Again I stare at her, weighing the wish to be right against the wish to be loving—and loved.

"I think I just want something to take the edge off when things get really crazy," she says and sips her wine.

"When are things not really crazy?" I ask, and T.J. shrugs.

"What's wrong with Paxil?" I ask, and T.J. shrugs again.

"Nothing's wrong with it," T.J. says. "I just don't want to live that way, that's all." She takes another sip of her wine. This may be Paxil-in-a-glass, but it doesn't require a prescription, and that means it doesn't require a shrink, and that means it doesn't require T.J. to admit what she doesn't want to admit.

"You mean you don't want to be happier?" I say.

"What I really want is just quiet," T.J. says. "And I want space to think."

This is as far as I can go.

If conversations are countries, then I have just come to a border, and beyond it, I know, lie dragons.

❋

Silently, I reach into my purse and take Mom's apartment keys out and pull off the extra copy.

"You can come here as often as you like," I tell her and hand her the key. Then I leave the room to start packing up the books that are on the front hallway shelves.

The next day at twilight, the windows in the buildings across the park turn orange in the setting sun. I have been working in the apartment since just before noon. I have long since achieved a rhythm, pulling books from the shelves and stacking them into piles, then kneeling beside the piles and sorting the books by size, then packing them like tangrams, geometric shapes with no spaces between them, order upon order.

What stops the rhythm I've created is a gray-and-red book that doesn't quite fit into any stack. It is called *The Anatomy of Happiness,* and it was written by a physician named Martin Gumpert. The copyright page says 1951, and the chapter list suggests an extremely prescient consideration of the links between mental and physical health.

I stay on the office floor, skimming the pages, rapt. And then, turning back to the beginning, I find on page four what the author calls simply "a prescription for happiness." In the margin beside this list are two thick, parallel, blue-penciled lines, as if someone long ago performed a benediction with inky fingers. This is the list, in its entirety:

1. Prevent physical suffering.
2. Prevent guilt.
3. Do not accept illusions.
4. Accept the reality of death.
5. Do what you like to do.
6. Keep learning.
7. Accept your limitations.

8. Be willing to pay for everything you get.

9. Be willing and able to love.

10. Avoid secrets.

I read and reread this list, as the darkness deepens beyond the living room windows. I try the list on and rearrange it, compare it to Freud, compare it to Aristotle. It seems at once both rigid and embracing, prescriptive but somehow forgiving.

A feathery breeze comes in through the windows and makes me feel unexpectedly calm. I stand up to look for the hallway light, not quite ready to return home or to leave the persuasive comfort of finding seeming wisdom by seeming chance.

I bring the book home that evening and add it to my stack of things to read. Directly underneath it is volume 47, number 1, of a journal called *Social Indicators Research: An International and Interdisciplinary Journal for Quality-of-Life Measurement*. Much of the issue is dedicated to an article entitled "Measuring the Well-beings of the Developing Countries." I open to a random page and read:

The achievement index for a particular indicator of well-being for a country at a point in time is:

$$A_{ij} = \frac{X_{ij} - X_{imin}}{X_{imax} - X_{imin}}$$

where X_{ij} = value of the ith indicator for jth country
X_{imin} = minimum value of the ith indicator
X_{imax} = maximum value of the ith indicator.

I close the journal.

I know this has something to do with happiness, but I also know there is no way in hell that I'll ever understand what.

I like the prescription book better, even if—as I'll later conclude—it seems based on the faulty premise that happiness can exist in anything like a constant state.

At ten o'clock the same evening, a dozen trunks and duffel bags are lined up in the lobby of our apartment building, waiting to be picked up by Camp Trucking, all labeled with camp names that sound like Indian tribes but are probably made from the first syllables of camp owners' parents' names.

I even feel my nose redden when I watch the trunks depart.

"Maybe I should get a dog," I say to Michael that night.

"You don't need a dog," he says, turning off our overhead light.

"They're really good to cuddle."

"So are husbands."

"They love you unconditionally."

"So do husbands," he says. "And you don't have to walk us."

"Maybe a cat," I say.

"Litter boxes."

"Maybe—"

"What you need," he tells me with unforgivable clarity, "cannot be purchased at a pet store."

I recall the website of an Orlando store called Happiness Is Pets.

"Maybe I should get a dog," I say to T.J. the next morning.

"Lot of work," she says.

"Maybe I should have a baby," I say.

She laughs. "Right, and that's less work."

"Why do you get to have three kids and I only get to have two?"

"Why do you get to have sex?"

"Why do you get to be famous?"

"Why do you get to have Michael?"

"Why do you get to work with Lucas?"

A pause, while she takes this in.

"She called me, you know."

"Marathon?"

"Yeah. She was totally embarrassed about the other night at the restaurant. Poor baby."

"You're so mean to her."

"Did you see that ring? It was in the window of Harry Winston's."

"You have no right to be jealous of Marathon Ross."

"You have no right to be flirting with Lucas Ross."

"I wasn't flirting," I say.

"Yeah, right," she says. "Has he called you?"

"What?"

"Have you called him?"

"Don't be ridiculous."

If he called me, I would say:

I don't do that sort of thing.

Thanks, but I'm not interested.

I'm flattered, but no thanks.

I would say:

I'm happily married.

I would say:

I have this empty apartment.

"He would make you miserable," T.J. says.

"Happiness isn't everything," I say.

12

> Happiness is nothing more than good
> health and a bad memory.
> —*Albert Schweitzer*

*S*aturday morning, the twenty-eighth of June, I wake up at five and lie in bed, unable to move and unable to go back to sleep. The buses aren't supposed to leave from Lincoln Center until eleven o'clock. To make matters worse, Michael is on call this weekend, his heartfelt attempts to trade gigs with another doctor having proved completely fruitless. So I spend the morning making French toast, and wrapping up sandwiches, and trying to keep the girls from adding yet more things to their bursting backpacks.

At ten o'clock, I stand at the bathroom mirror with Emily and brush her hair for the last time in eight weeks. I shudder at the thought of what the girls will look like after even eight days, and I blame myself again for not having insisted on radical hair-cuts.

"Ouch," Emily says now, as I make her braids too tight.

"Sorry," I say.

Emily tries to pull away. "You're hurting me, Mom," she says, in an almost whine.

"Well, just think: you won't have to do this with me for two whole months," I say and hate myself immediately. It is wrong, it is all wrong to try to make her feel guilty for leaving, and I know it. How could I not know it? It isn't her fault that she hasn't discovered a way to stop time.

"You'll do a great job with your own hair," I say now briskly, trying to cover.

"Did you pack the new hair elastics?"

"Yes, sweetie. You did it with me."

"In the trunk?"

"Yes, in the trunk."

"And it'll be there when we get there?"

"Yes."

"And the key?"

"You have the key in your backpack."

"Oh, Mommy," Emily says and turns around to hug me, hard.

"You'll be fine, sweetheart," I whisper to the shiny, sweet top of Emily's head. "I know you'll be fine, I know it," I say and can just imagine her on a shrink's couch someday, saying, "It was the day I left for summer camp. I was totally fine about it until my mother started sobbing."

And so on I trudge, into a hot, gray morning, with a smile fixed on my face like a scar.

The bus pulls out precisely and mercifully on schedule. Emily and Katie wave good-bye in brave, tank-topped unison. I stand by amid a swell of diesel exhaust fumes, hoping the bus's grimy windows will obscure the fact that tears are now coursing down my cheeks. I keep my smile firmly in place, hoping it will fool the girls, if not the mothers around me, and I put off reaching for the telltale Kleenex until the bus is well out of sight.

Then, tearful and unseeing, I feel for the wad of tissues that I stuffed into my handbag at the last moment.

"First time?" I hear a voice say, and there is Abbie Prynn, standing beside me in dignified blondness.

I manage to nod.

"You'll see," she says. "They'll love it."

"I didn't know that Celia went to Sha-no-Wah," I say, suppressing a lingering sob.

"For years," Abbie says.

"For *years*?"

"Well, since she was seven," Abbie says.

"She's been going to sleepaway camp since she was *seven*?"

Abbie nods with what seems to be unfeigned nonchalance.

"She loved it from the start," she says.

I manage to smile and, more important, manage not to shout "Who *are* you? Are you *crazy*?"

"Have a good summer," I say instead.

"You too."

And I turn to walk home, as slowly as I possibly can. I don't want to be alone just now, but Abbie's presence makes me feel not less but more so.

I come home to find a bulky manila envelope postmarked South Carolina and addressed to me in a slightly shaky hand. The note inside is written in the usual underscored capital letters:

SALLY. I <u>CLIPPED</u> THESE PICTURES FOR <u>YOU</u>. THOUGHT THEY MIGHT GIVE YOU SOME <u>INSPIRATION</u>.

Enclosed are pages torn from various shelter magazines—some evidently quite old—with neon-colored Post-it arrows pointing to a couch here or a fabric there, a lamp, a bookcase.

What exactly does she want me to do with these?

"Mom," I say to her on the phone. "Do you realize you're talking about icing a cake and I'm still talking about trying to find some eggs?"

"That reminds me," she says with classic Mom logic. "I want to thank the girls for their birthday cards. Put them on."

"I can't," I say, once more fighting the lump in my throat. "I just put them on the bus for camp."

"Oh, good," she says expansively. "Then you'll really be able to get the place done."

Michael has made reservations at one of our favorite neighborhood restaurants, his intention clearly being to celebrate our first childless night since Emily's birth. For this event, he has come straight from the hospital with a look of expectant pleasure.

I am wearing a summer dress and trying to match his benign expression. In fact I am feeling something akin to first-date nervousness, and the questions cavorting through my mind are vaguely retrograde: Will we have things in common? Will we laugh? Will there be awkward pauses? Who is this man, anyway, when he is not my partner in parenthood? It's as if Sears and Roebuck suddenly had to talk about something other than retail.

Together we sit at a table by the window, next to a row of clay pots filled with tall, silly, bright grass.

Across the avenue, I can see into the window of a babyGap, where five tiny mannequins frolic in sandals and beach clothes.

"What is it?" Michael asks me.

"Nothing," I say. "How'd it go at the hospital?"

"Fine. What are you looking at?"

"Nothing."

I open my menu. "What are you having?" I ask him.

He looks out the window, finding my view.

"They'll be fine," he tells me.

"I know they'll be fine."

He is missing the point.

"Emily may be a little homesick at first, but she'll get used to it. It'll be good for her. And Katie will be in heaven."

"I know."

How can he not understand that I am sad not for them but for myself?

"What, then?"

"I am not worrying about the girls," I say.

I look out the window again.

"Talk to me," Michael says.

On cue, a pregnant woman stops in front of the Gap window.

How can Michael not know? How can he, of all people, not understand that onto that bus and into that awful, gray, diesely morning, the girls have taken not only their backpacks and their courage but also, irrevocably, my youth?

I force myself to smile, but what I feel most is trapped by his clinical stare. Then his stare turns angry.

"For almost a decade, you've been saying that all you need is a little time and space so that you can get some work done," he says.

I nod.

"Now you're going to have time and space. The kids will be out of your hair all summer. You'll have the whole place to yourself every day."

I nod.

"You're going to write a great book," Michael tells me.

"And then what?"

"Then you'll write another."

"I'll be in my forties," I tell him.

"You're already in your forties."

"Thank you."

"You'll be in your forties if you have another baby," he says.

"But I'll be too busy to notice," I say.

"You do realize that's ridiculous."

"I don't really think I want another baby," I say.

"I know."

"I just want—I don't think I know."

Actually, I do think I know. At this moment, I think what I want is to feel the way I did when Lucas Ross reached for my hand under the table. At this moment, I think all I want is for Lucas Ross to paint me. To fuck me. To shock me.

"Don't be so far away," Michael says now, in the wise, knowing, loving, true tone of voice that makes me want to go screaming out into the night.

He wants to have sex as soon as we get home. A locked door and a willing look are usually all Michael needs to inspire him. Even at the age of forty-two, he seems to live in a perpetual state of sexual semireadiness. But tonight, we don't even have to lock a door. Tonight, for the first time since we became parents, we have the whole place entirely to ourselves.

He leads me excitedly from room to room, as if we are thinking of buying the place.

He settles, with a playful grin, on the living room couch. He motions to me to lie down on him.

"You're sure," I say.

"Come here," he says. "Allow me to remind you," he says, "what happiness is."

Later, after he brings us two large glasses of ice water, I say: "What *do* you think it is?"

"Happiness?"

I nod.

"You don't know what I think it is?" Michael asks me.

"Sex?" I say.

"It's this minute."

I laugh.

"No. Really," he says, almost angrily. "It's *this* conversation. *This* night."

"What are you saying?" I ask him.

"It's *this* dinner," he says, sitting up. "It's *this* night. It's having the girls *this* age. It's us being married *this* long. It's *this* minute. Happiness is *this* minute."

I am moved by the force of his certainty. And for a moment, I almost allow myself to think that he is right.

I try to sleep late the next morning, but I can't. I wake up at six and lie in bed, tired but racing, my thoughts bounding from Katie to Emily and back again.

Rationally, I know that they will be fine. Rationally, I know that I will be fine (actually, what I know is that I will be old and, eventually, dead, but other than that I will be fine). But here is what I am thinking: Did Emily cry last night? Cling to someone? Sleep at all? Did Katie boast and posture, as she does most when she's scared? Should I have even sent them? And where is the benefit of an empty nest if it's so filled with worry?

In a sense, I have been dreading this day for ten years, ever since a nurse took the seconds-old Emily, screaming, to be weighed and measured and I, still raw in every sense from the act of giving birth, wept at the shock of the separation. Now, a decade later, it is not so much that I adore or embrace every aspect of motherhood. It is simply that I cannot imagine myself functioning any other way.

Motherhood has, in a sense, existed apart from whatever paths to happiness—domestic, professional, marital—I have tried to construct or follow. Yet motherhood has not exactly been a different road, or even a detour. It has been more like a different weather system on the same road, a system that changed nothing and changed everything. Motherhood has alternately clouded, brightened, warmed, and frozen me, perked me up and knocked me down. And despite my best efforts, it has landed me here, panic-stricken, at 6:00 A.M., with happiness starting to seem like something necessarily confined to the past.

Michael wakes at seven. Our first weekend alone should be a festival of lingering brunches and rediscovered sexual acts, but the contrasting realities are: (1) that he is still on call, and (2) that I am secretly grateful that he is still on call. So I stay in bed, pretending to concentrate on the Sunday *Times* while he showers and dresses and goes to work.

How can happiness be *this moment* if *this moment* sucks?

With nervous conviction, I spend Sunday at my desk, trying to figure out where and when happiness first became an end in itself. Back in the Middle Ages, when rewards could be had only in heaven, personal happiness was at best a dubious prospect. In a time pervaded by Christian morality, too much joy or worldly success could only mean you had failed somehow to sacrifice and serve. The Protestant ideal changed this somewhat by making worldly rewards seem like a promise of greater rewards to come. But a Cotton Mather or William Bradford could still never have understood happiness as an end in itself. Happiness for its own sake would have made no more sense to either of them than suffering for its own sake.

Does either of them make sense to me? Right now, perhaps till I hear from the girls, it seems that nothing makes sense to me.

Monday's mail brings only magazines and bills.

Mercifully, on Tuesday, I find two letters in the mailbox when I come home from the library, and I don't even put my bag down before I start to open the first of them. I read:

> *Dear Mom and Dad,*
>   *Camp is great! I love my Bunk! We are called the*

*Robins. We get to swim twice a day! Celia is here. She has a
bra! I love you! Please send cookies!*

> *Katie*

Katie's handwriting is large and fast and forward slanting. Her ex-
clamation points bounce across the page like musical notes.

I sit down to read the letter from Emily:

Dear Mom and Dad,
 *I miss you. The trip was fine. The first night was hard. I
couldn't sleep and I was crying. I miss you. All the girls here
know each other from last year and the year before. They've
got all these jokes and they have nicknames, like everyone is
called something "eeny." There's a girl named Lucy and
she's Luceeny. There's a girl named Tina and she's Tineeny. I
figured out that I would be Emileeny. But no one has called
me that.*
 *Well, that's all for now. I just saw Katie at lineup for
dinner, and she was fine.*
 I miss you.
 Love,
 Emily

> *P.S. Celia has a bra!*

Beyond the living room windows I can just make out a couple
on the roof across the way as they set out plates for a barbecue. I
recall when Michael and I climbed up to the roof of this building
for a picnic dinner. That was ages ago, before the girls, of course.
It seems ancient now. I want to scream at the couple: Just wait! Just
wait till you get married and you have children and your daughter
is miserable because her bunkmates won't give her a nickname!

There is Emily, game but grim, and there is Katie, ever gleeful, in response to the same situation.

And there is Aristotle, who said you couldn't be happy without being good, and there is Emily, who is so good, and so unhappy. And Katie, who doesn't care if she is good but seems to be happy. And Michael. Happy and good, and totally in the dark about how it is to be anything else.

And I, who am anything else.

I wait one more day, and then I call Lucas from my cell phone.

"Yes?" he says when he picks up the phone.

I might have guessed that he was the kind of person to answer his phone this way. It makes me laugh, but nervously.

"Yes?" Lucas says again.

"Hello," I say. "It's Sally Farber."

And Dr. Martin Gumpert's "prescription for happiness" list pops into my mind.

Prevent physical suffering.

No, I think, I will not suffer physically, not unless he is far kinkier than I imagine.

Prevent guilt.

Am I guilty? Emphatically, if inexplicably, I am not guilty.

"Sally," Lucas says now, as if he is saying "chocolate torte."

"Did you think I would call you?" I ask him, with more confidence than I can remember having felt in months, if not years.

"No," he says, but somehow this doesn't faze me.

"Did you want me to call you?" I ask him.

Do not accept illusions.

He will never love me. Never. He will never, ever, love me.

And it will never be right to sleep with him. It will never be justifiable, not by anything Michael has done to me, or failed to do—not even by the old, remorseless gift of his perfection.

"Yes, of course I wanted you to call me," he says huskily.

"But you weren't going to call me."

"I'm not good at cajoling."

"Should I ask you now what you *are* good at?"

He laughs. "Oh, I'm going to like this," he says.

Accept the reality of death.

Yes, I think. What the hell, I think. We're all going to die anyway.

Do what you like to do.

"I have this apartment," I tell Lucas, and as I do so, I run my hand along my left shin, testing for smoothness.

And so I never get to the end of the list, and the part about not keeping secrets.

13

Happiness is the light on the water.
The water is cold and dark and deep.
—*William Maxwell*

My father died my junior year in college. He had no illness, no warning, and no premonition. One day, I had a father, and the next day, I had a story to tell.

My father was an advertising man, and on a mild October morning, he went to the Park Avenue offices of a prospective client to pitch a new campaign. He was standing at the head of the ebony conference table in the company's boardroom, and he had just taken out his storyboards when the ceiling above him literally caved in and a huge air-conditioning duct crushed him to death. No one else was killed. No one else was even injured.

The client was a famous cosmetics company that was trying to introduce a glow-in-the-dark lipstick.

Now when people asked me what my father did, I had to say that my father was dead, and because I was only nineteen, that always provoked pity and curiosity, and I would have to tell the story about the ceiling caving in. Then I would have to watch as people invariably seemed to measure their chances of ever being in the boardroom of a major cosmetics company and having a ceiling fall in on them.

Happiness, in those days, in the days after the funeral, when I was back at college trying to study, was an intellectual construct, and that was all it was.

Every evening when the sun began to set and my roommates went to eat in the house cafeteria, I would feel walls of panic rise around me, and I would know that there was no way that I would be able to eat with them, let alone to speak, and I would go downstairs and get a tray and go to the salad bar. I would get a scoop of egg salad, and two slices of thick brown bread, and tomatoes and lettuce, and I would take the tray back up to my room and turn on the eight-inch-square black-and-white Sony television set that I had been given, as a matter of fact, by my father. The knob had fallen off long before, and the channels had to be turned now with a pair of pliers. But I would find, every night at seven o'clock, the reruns of *M*A*S*H*, and only then, my mind completely soothed by the rhythm and reliability of that show, would I be able to eat.

*M*A*S*H* wasn't comforting because it made me think that if those wacky doctors and nurses could survive the Korean War then I could survive my father's death. It wasn't comforting because of the evidence of humor in the face of adversity. It was comforting only because, at the beginning of every episode, something would happen that would make everyone more unhappy, and by the end of the episode, something else would happen that would make everyone less unhappy, and they all would return to stasis, and it didn't matter that their stasis was an unstable one. The world had, once again, righted itself. That gave me some measure of peace, or at least of distraction.

After the show was over, I would stack my tray on top of the others I'd not yet had the energy to return to the cafeteria, and I would attempt to do my schoolwork. That fall, I was taking, among other subjects, an advanced course in English poetry, and I was reading—and reading and reading, because there was no end to him—Tennyson. His famous poem "In Memoriam," which before my father's death had seemed the longest, most self-indulgent, least rewarding document in the English language, now teemed with the knowledge of loss and the promise of wisdom. I said "Hah!" bitterly and out loud when I read the lines " 'Tis better to have loved and lost / Than never to have loved at all," but I allowed myself, for at least a moment, to think that, if it had worked for Tennyson, then it might work for me.

By eleven o'clock, I would get into bed and turn on the TV again, and there would be another episode of *M*A*S*H,* with its sweet sitcom comfort, and I would fall asleep with the TV on.

This is all that happiness was to me then: the absence of pain. Happiness was the dim, short, black-and-white corridor between Hawkeye Pierce and sleep.

I rarely saw Michael that fall or winter. He had come to New York for the funeral, an act that touched me deeply, because I had not even asked him to, and in fact I had not even spoken to him. We had not been boyfriend and girlfriend since the previous spring, and I had treated him terribly then, and I had treated him terribly since. He had decided to go premed anyway, and when I did see him, he was sleepless and, I thought, a little too self-important.

Paul was the man of the hour then or, more accurately, the man of the semester. Paul was tall, strong, and angular, a party boy but with soul. What I remember about Paul after my father's death is that I wanted him to know me, to understand me, and to keep me safe. What I remember is that he wanted to run for the hills and that he was too decent to do so, but not too decent to keep me from knowing how decent he was to stay.

This, then, was what I imagined:

In the dead of winter, seeing my breath before me, I took a step across the street, then faltered, weaving, faint. Paul, who had just left my side, turned back to look for me. On my face was a flash of apology. On his was horror and dread. As I started to fall, the car came around the corner before he could reach me. It hit me, and I flew into the air. I flipped over and came back down, landing dully on the hood of the car, the back of my head crashing through the windshield, which shattered but held, a spider's web.

I was still conscious. As a crowd gathered around the car, Paul screamed: "Call an ambulance! Don't move her! Don't touch her!"

He knelt beside me on the hood of the car. My face was bleeding profusely from my many cuts. If the windshield gave way, I would of course have more.

Paul took my hand.

"I think your life depends on staying still," he told me.

I acknowledged what he said with my eyes.

"Can you tell me what hurts most?" he asked me, and his eyes showed the depth of his guilt about not having loved me more.

"My head," I said, my eyes blurry.

My legs were twisted into terrible shapes.

"Can you feel your legs?" he asked me gently.

"I can't feel them," I said, and then panic and pain engulfed me.

❄

I had this fantasy, or versions of it, for the entire fall and winter after my father died. At first, it was just a shower thought, or a walking-to-my-next-class thought. But soon it replaced the sitcom as my way of getting to sleep. Every night now, even on nights when I fell asleep beside Paul, I would embroider this tale in my mind: another injury, a different location, but always the look of love and guilt overwhelming the passivity in Paul's face. Always the dream of rescue. Of safety in a strong man's arms.

Then the fantasy of injury and rescue gave way to something else.

By now it was late December, and the prospect of Christmas vacation loomed empty, long, and bleak: home to my mourning, shell-shocked mother, and the burden of being her only comfort, and the knowledge that she was supposed to be mine. Paul would be going home to Detroit, none too relieved to escape my grief.

On the day that the last of our midterms was over, I assumed we would have a night of celebration, or at least a night of sex, but when I got back to my dorm room from my exam, I saw no note from Paul. I went to his dorm room, which was three floors away, and I found him packing his bag.

Of course, life had just betrayed me, grabbing my father at the age of fifty-five. Life had just revealed itself to be bent and bizarre. But that betrayal was momentarily dwarfed by the betrayal of Paul packing his bags for a Christmas at home without me. I remember literally sinking to my knees in amazement and loneliness.

That night, the first stroke made a simple white line. It was a gesture, a sketch, not unlike the marks an artist makes in charcoal before he starts a painting.

After the first stroke, the work began. The scratches, back and forth, with a single index finger. Not too deep. Not too hard. Just no interruptions, and then it barely hurt at all.

It took a full five minutes before any blood showed, and then it wasn't blood that gushed or ran but rather just streaked yellow and red where I'd rubbed the skin away.

It only hurt when I stopped, and then it stung like the end of the world.

My mother never saw the cut. We were together, over Christmas vacation, every day for three weeks, and at first I had a huge, index-card-sized Band-Aid on my forearm, and then I had the cut itself, the size and shape of a large caterpillar, crusting over now, its back scab-brown, its edges still slightly yellow.

It was big and disgusting and unavoidable, and she managed for three weeks not to see it.

Later I would forgive her, but that was only after I was married and could shudder at the image of a ceiling falling on Michael.

At the time, I endured her neglect with outward stoicism and private frenzy. I made more cuts: on my feet, my legs, the backs of my hands, my other arm. It was not ostensibly her attention I was seeking, though. It was Paul's.

By the time I returned to college, I had eight or ten cuts like that on my body, and after not hearing from Paul for the first two days back, I was fairly sure that he wasn't going to see the cuts I'd made either.

It was Michael who saw the cuts first. They were almost completely healed by then. The first one, on my left arm, was already a white scar, hardly noticeable. He noticed it anyway.

Somehow, I expected him to know, instantly, that I'd made these cuts myself, and somehow he did. But he didn't scold me, not even once, not even later, and that I had not expected.

He traced, with affection I never knew could be alluring too, the light white skin on my forearm, and he kissed the spot just above it.

"Oh, sweetheart," he said, which was the first time that anyone had ever called me *sweetheart*.

I tried to shrug myself away, even though I wanted him near me.

"If I could be with you, you'd never need to do something like this," he said, and for the next two decades, more or less, he would turn out to have been right.

14

> What we call happiness in the strictest sense comes
> from the (preferably sudden) satisfaction of needs
> which have been dammed up to a high degree.
> —*Sigmund Freud*

I saw a shrink for three years, and once, she asked me what it was that I really wanted to be, and I said I thought what I really wanted to be was happy.

And then the shrink said, "Happy?"

And I said, "Yes. Happy."

And the shrink said, "Talk about *happy*. What does *happy* mean to you?"

And I was alarmed but looked at the shrink calmly and said, "It means *happy*. What does it mean to you?"

"I'm interested," the shrink said, "in knowing what it means to you."

"It means happy," I said. "Happy. You know. Not depressed. Not miserable. Not lonely. Not sad."

"And so," she said with great portent, "you are choosing to define happiness as the absence of something."

"Yes," I answered slowly. "I am choosing to define happiness as the absence of unhappiness."

There was a long and seemingly important silence. But in it, I was attempting to calculate how much money I had spent on therapy and what I might be able to buy if I quit.

Maybe a chair that wasn't stuffed with feathers whose pointy ends were always finding their way through the fabric and into my legs.

Now *that* would make me happy.

Unhappiness is a relative state, somewhat akin to pain, or misfortune. The knowledge of its scale rarely helps. Rationally, you can know the difference between a broken toe and a broken skull, but if you're the one with the broken toe, you won't feel less pain when you see someone with a broken skull. You'll only feel more guilt and—unless you're hopelessly insensitive—talk about your pain less freely.

Rationally, I can know the difference between sadness and tragedy, loss and deprivation, remorse and regret. Intellectually, I can know that, with the exception of my father's death, I have never really had any legitimate cause to be unhappy.

But that doesn't keep me happy.

On my better days, however, it does make me try.

One autumn morning years ago I ran into a mother in Emily's nursery school class, and when I asked her how her summer had been, she told me about the sudden departure of her children's babysitter.

"This is the worst thing that has ever happened to me," the woman told me, without sarcasm or apology.

And indeed, the women I know all seem to indulge and exaggerate life's woes. We are always granting ourselves small favors, as if completely immune to the larger ones that fate has already granted us.

"I just had to do something for myself." That is one of T.J.'s favorite lines, offered by way of explanation for a new handbag or a manicure. Offered with unapologetic pride in the fact that she has put herself first. As if T.J.'s entire life hasn't been systematically constructed by and for herself, a skyscraper of choices that she nonetheless manages to disown at each higher floor.

And yet. Here am I, no different, no better, with a thirst that I seem unable to quench. And if thirst doesn't exactly qualify as unhappiness, it doesn't seem to qualify as happiness, either.

George Bernard Shaw wrote that the only way to avoid unhappiness was not to have enough leisure time in which to wonder if you were happy or not.

It may be that time—despite all our protests and attempts to dull it down—is really the most embarrassing luxury we have.

ARE YOU SUFFERING FROM HAPPINESS ANXIETY?

This is the headline for a column about weight loss that I read online. "Experts say this is a feeling of stress or anxiety as we reach our goals . . ."

Faced only with a demanding mother and a healthy book contract and a genetically happy husband and two nice but absent children and an unringing telephone, I force myself to think about the women on the *Mayflower*.

On the prairie.

In the Civil War.

In the Holocaust.

I think about Posey Rivers, with her hyuk-hyuk laugh in the courtyard and her cigarette-burned hand.

These were women whose chief goal was survival, and who never spent time brooding about how much or how little they should work. Women whose strength made them beautiful, fearless, and—in my mind—always high-cheekboned. Women who never talked about—and no doubt never even had—insomnia, or PMS, or hair on their legs.

Imagine settling Plymouth Colony with a weekly trip to the shrink.

Imagine Abigail Adams saying: "I just had to do something for myself."

It is not that I think having an affair with Lucas Ross will be smart, or right, or even marginally justifiable. It is simply that it has become all I can think about wanting to do, the way that cutting my arm or my hand once seemed all I could think about wanting to do. And really—though I won't find this out until later—for much the same reason.

On Friday night, settling into bed beside Michael, I read in Aristotle:

> But what constitutes happiness is a matter of dispute; and the popular account of it is not the same as that given by the philosophers . . .

And I think: What if what constitutes happiness is sex with a famous artist who understands sadness and depth and ambition?

Aristotle writes:

> Now perhaps it would be a somewhat fruitless task to review all the different opinions that are held . . .

And I think: You may be onto something there, fella.

But then Monday morning, Michael goes off to the hospital,

and the phone rings, and it is finally Lucas, and I give him the address of Mom's apartment, and I go to get my hair cut and to have my legs waxed.

The Bishop Salon, on West Fifty-seventh Street, is one of those deceptively seedy Manhattan establishments whose generally rundown appearance belies its prices and its clientele. I have been having my hair cut here since the month before my wedding, when T.J. insisted that a makeover was due.

"It's all about this, honey," Antonio said to me once, waving his comb toward the mirror. "This is what makes them all crazy, honey. I'm telling you. Believe me. I have seen dogs, I mean pooches, little schnauzers, and I don't know what they see in that thing but they carry themselves like Grace Kelly. And then you see these women who are all hunched over, no self-confidence. Who even *knows* what they look like? They do everything they can to avoid being seen. And they can't look in the mirror at all."

Today, I have brought protection from the mirror, in the form of an article to read, but my concentration is invaded by snippets of beauty parlor conversation:

"So Margaret says she basically only likes to do it when the weather's good. Well, she gets these hideous migraines, you know, and she thinks it has something to do with the rain . . ."

And from another corner. "See what you can do with the top of it. I'm starting to look like David Bowie."

And from another: "He said, 'You're being a bitch.' And I said, 'No, darling, I'm absolutely nothing like this when I'm being a bitch.'"

The leg waxing provides the perfect blend of decorative self-indulgence and brutal self-torture.

I lie on the table in one of the salon's back rooms, tracing the wallpaper pattern with my eyes and inhaling the slightly tropical smell of perfumed, heated wax. A heavy-set Russian woman named

Anya smoothes the hot goo onto my legs, then flattens it with a strip of cloth and rips the hairs out. She asks questions in a Natasha cartoon accent but mercifully, after five or ten minutes, lapses into silence.

In that silence, I think of my girls, incomprehensibly distant. Their absence seems to define me now, just as their presence has done since their births. The sounds of their games and laughter and fights. Their breath, their mess, their puzzles, their projects. Their sweatshirts and rain slickers piled on the floor of their closet in tangled embraces.

I had not imagined what it would really be like to have all that gone, just as, before their births, I hadn't been able to picture the gorgeous chaos they would bring.

I wonder about Emily's nightmares, and about Katie's hair.

Lying on my back now, I watch the small red dots rise on my thighs as the wax is pulled off. I like the way I'll feel when this is finished: smooth and female, like a girl on a date. And that is what I have today. My first date in more than twenty years.

For some reason the leg waxing always hurts me most around my ankles, and I wince and feel my muscles tighten as Anya reaches them now.

"Okay for you?" Anya asks.

Unaccountably, tears come to my eyes.

"Missus?" Anya asks.

"It's okay," I say.

"I hurt you?" Anya asks.

"No, it's okay," I say.

"Take deep breath," she says, then tears off another strip of wax.

Staring now at the overhead light in the ceiling, I feel the tears sliding down the sides of my cheeks and all the way around to the back of my neck. Mortified by my own childishness, I am nonetheless unable to stop. I feel ugly, and that makes me cry; I have a date with a stranger, and that makes me cry; I haven't seen my children for more than a week, and that makes me cry; and I am crying, and that makes me cry.

"Missus?" Anya asks again and hands me a tissue.

I wipe my eyes.

"Missus? I stop now."

There is still a patch of unwaxed hair by my left ankle. It is ridiculous, I think, to leave it there, and yet I cannot stop crying, and I know that I will not be able to stop crying until I have cried much more.

"Yes," I finally say. "Please stop now."

Anya looks sincerely perplexed, if not a little annoyed. "I bring you something?" she asks me.

I shake my head.

"You get rest," Anya finally says, helplessly, as she picks up her bucket of wax and backs out of the room.

Sobbing now in the cool solitude of the wallpapered, flowery room, I hug my knees to my chest and stare relentlessly at the one unmanicured patch on my leg.

Two hours later, Lucas Ross thrusts his tongue into my mouth and then waits, unmoving, waits as if it should be enough for me to have some part of him inside some part of me. I have never had someone kiss me like this. It is not really kissing, actually; it is more of a presentation, an entrance. There his tongue is, inside my mouth, firm, smooth, waiting, totemic. And so I have to move, to make him move, because worship is not my only intention. But I wonder, as I kiss him and as, gradually, my kisses make him kiss me back, if it will be like this in bed. Will he make me move by not moving? Will he make me crazy with waiting? Is this some bizarre, bewitching technique, or is it just ego, only his ego, saying: *Here I am, dance around me; celebrate me, make me move?*

But it is new, oh, God, it is so new. It is only a kiss, and it is so new. It explodes, engages, and tenses me. It dissolves me, and makes me want more.

"Sally, my God, you're delicious," he says, just at the moment when I am starting to wonder if he has any idea who I am.

It is so much easier than I thought it would be. Such a silly (SILLY ?) circle, it seems, to draw around ourselves all these years. Cross this line and you are guilty. In fact, I feel not guilty when I come home but sexy and strong and fine. My hour with Lucas was just an hour: I spent longer getting my hair cut and my legs waxed.

I just had to do something for myself. T.J. gets manicures, and I get laid.

This is what I think I am thinking.

In fact, I am giddy with loss.

15

To fill the hour—that is happiness, to fill the hour and
leave no crevice for a repentance or an approval.
—*Ralph Waldo Emerson*

*I*t is July, and the heat has descended on New York City like a
form of pestilence. Air conditioners drip onto sidewalks. Tar on
the pavement melts. Women who have spent the spring months
running conspicuous laps around Central Park retreat to the air-
conditioned comfort of their gyms, where they devote extra time
to working on their upper arms.

At home, dust settles on my neglected computer. At my mother's
apartment, I find a rusted standing fan in the back of the bedroom
closet, but when I get up the nerve to plug it in, it only gags and
wheezes and barely circulates the ancient air. At the local hardware

store, I finally order three small air conditioners and make an appointment to have them installed.

I reason that air-conditioning will help me sell the apartment at some point, but really my true objective is to make sure Lucas is comfortable. From our very first minutes at the apartment, he has shown not the slightest reluctance to tell me exactly when and how he isn't.

"Is this what you call a drink?" he asked me.

"Is that what you call a greeting?"

"Is this heat some form of punishment?"

The questions sting me and make my heart race, but the feelings are not entirely bad. Lucas, I quickly discover, can be spoiled, demanding, and mean, but he is so clearly in charge that I feel almost relieved. Things, it is clear, will be done according to Lucas's plans or not done at all. I have no vote, no voice, no power. If the building is burning down and Lucas wants to stay, I will never be able to get him to leave. This is surprisingly soothing. It is comfortable—and perhaps in my childhood home it is also somehow inevitable—to have someone else in charge.

"I can't see you less than once a week," he declares at the end of our second date.

I laugh. It is so clear he's done this before. I feel like a Scout being taught the secret salute.

"What's funny?"

"Yes, sir," I say.

"Well, I can't. I can't see you less than once a week," he says again.

"I guess I should ask you why," I say.

"Because show me a form of therapy that works if you do it less than once a week."

"I'm your therapy?"

"How about Tuesday mornings?"

I am flattered but don't want to show it. "Could we start with just next Tuesday?" I ask.

He kisses me.

"And maybe the one after that?" I say.

"Now you're getting the point," he says. He checks his watch and pulls his enormous gray T-shirt back on.

"Aren't you going to tell me the rest?" I ask him.

"Mmm? The rest of what?"

"How this is just a fling? How no one must ever know?"

"Okay," he says congenially, bending down to put on a sneaker. He wears black Converse All Stars, which make him look like a *New Yorker* cartoon. "No one must ever know."

"Lucas."

"All right," he says. "To be honest, I wouldn't want you telling your friend T.J., because she's liable to tell her friend Marathon, and wives are generally not too understanding about this sort of thing."

"Aren't you at all concerned about whether this is going to mean more to me than to you?" I ask him.

"Oh, I assume it will," he says cheerfully and without hesitation. And then, with bone-crushing charm, "simply because I'm a selfish shit and you're a goddamned miraculous angel."

He kisses me vibrantly and smiles all the way out the door.

Apart from anything else, I now have fresh incentive to want to get Mom's place into shape. Not only do I have a new in-house critic—You call this a chair? You call this a wall?—but I also have a reason to want to make the place my own. Specifically, I need access to a nondisgusting shower where I can wash away my guilt with soap and shampoo.

Not that I'm all that guilty.

But on Friday the eleventh I show up with a few towels and washcloths, soaps, a bath mat, and many toiletries—and am startled to find T.J. already well ensconced.

What surprises me is not her presence—I had remembered, even the first time with Lucas, that I'd given her a key—but that she has somehow achieved a proprietary air.

It takes me a moment to realize why, and then it is all too clear: T.J. is talking on the telephone when I walk in. The telephone that, up until now, I had not had reconnected. And she is talking to her office, which makes her sound even more like an owner. She is issuing orders and sighs and has about her a look of power and direction and proficiency that I find vaguely terrifying.

As I walk in, she motions to me grandly that she'll be off in a second, and for a moment I want to lunge across the desk at her beautiful, talented, competent neck. She points me toward a stack of magazines that she has spread like a fan on one of the doctor's filing cabinets.

Laid out before me are issues of *Elle Decor, House Beautiful, Architectural Digest,* and *Metropolitan Home.*

"I don't care if he's hit a block," she is saying, "we still have a deadline."

Yellow Post-it notes adorn the tops and sides of these magazines like fringe.

"I *know* he's got a show coming up," she says, and I freeze. "I've got a print run coming up. No. I know. It's not your fault," she says. "But see what you can do."

She hangs up, exasperated, powerful. "Artists!" she shouts, then leans back and unbuttons her jacket. "That was your boyfriend's agent."

"My what?"

"Lucas," she says. But she doesn't know anything, and though I know I will eventually tell her everything, I am not prepared to tell her yet. I calculate the odds of her walking in on any given Tuesday morning. I calculate the odds that a locked top lock will work to deter her. The odds, in either case, do not favor my keeping this a secret. But for the time being I want to try anyway, which actually gives me my first inkling that I may be more serious about this than I thought.

"Why didn't you ask me if you could connect the phone?" I say to her quietly.

She shrugs, opening her bag and pulling out a package of long pretzel sticks. "I've got to get a better cell. My battery keeps dying. Don't worry. I'll pay for it."

She takes one of the pretzel sticks and puts it in her mouth, a salted cigar.

"Want one?" she says, and I take one. "You'll see," she says. "It'll come in handy. The phone, I mean. And we've got to get some air conditioners in here. I mean, it's a sauna."

"I've ordered them," I say, and I think of Lucas's chest hairs, sparkly with sweat, sea foam at high tide.

"Good girl!" T.J. says, with annoying enthusiasm and condescension. "Now," she continues, pointing again to the filing cabinet, "see what I brought you?"

"You have spent more money on these magazines," I tell her, "than I intend to spend on the entire redecoration."

"Oh, don't be ridiculous."

"You just don't want me to write this book, right?"

"What are you talking about? The whole point is that if you hire Marathon, then you won't have to do all this yourself."

I know there is no way I am ever going to let that woman set foot in the place where I have just started having raucous sex with her husband. But at the moment, in a rash spirit of optimism, I allow myself to believe that T.J. is less persistent than she is.

"Does she have any experience?" I ask, pretending I care a little.

"She's got great taste," T.J. says firmly. "In everything except men."

❋

In the afternoon, I try new beginnings.

Happiness is a mirror. Far more than fear, anger, pride, or love, it is a reflection of a reality that differs completely from person to person.

I miss the days of the typewriter, when a page could be ripped out, noisily, and crumpled into a fixed, hard ball.

Happiness is an ocean.
A tree.
A flower.
A taco.
Happiness is freedom.
Is goodness.
Is balance.
Is peace.

Happiness is the subject of the book I am trying but failing to write.

At night, Michael and I sit in bed side by side, our notebook computers resting on our stomachs.

I write:

In the last decade, a number of researchers in fields ranging from psychology to economics have begun to document the rather noticeable gap between what people think will make them happy and what actually does make them happy. The findings reveal that material possessions are far less likely to increase happiness than social interactions are.

Yet more startling than any specific mistake people make in their predictions is the frequency with which their predictions are wrong. The reason, these researchers hypothesize, is that human beings are designed to be adaptive, so that—as shameful as it might seem from a certain perspective—it is perfectly natural to get used to the new house you worked so hard to buy and then, fairly quickly, start to think it needs improvements, or, more likely, to notice it not at all. Rising expectations are just another way of staying human, which is to say remaining a striving, ambitious, demanding, desiring, acquiring, pursuing beast.

Surreptitiously, I scan Michael's face now, searching in vain for a single surprise. I know I should feel guilty and scared about Lucas, but I don't. What I feel instead is oddly defiant, as if Michael's failure to guess what I'm doing gives me more license to do it.

I move on to solitaire, soothed by the calculable rewards of order and resolution and, whenever I lose, the all-important chance to click on the option "Replay Game."

Michael reviews a patient's history and taps out instructions to himself. On the shelf, the TV mutely flashes the emerald green of the Yankees' outfield. It is as if we are taking part in some electronic worship ceremony, with the triangle of the three monitors casting strange light.

I try to imagine what this scene is like in the Ross homestead. Lucas Ross muttering "He was safe" to the TV screen? Marathon hoping for the seven of clubs? Somehow, I don't think so.

"Cookie!" Jimmy Shannon shouts on the phone when he calls the next morning.

"Jimmy," I say. "It's Saturday."

"Right you are, Cookie," he chirps. "I'm well aware of that."

"Jimmy. It's a Saturday morning in July. Don't tell me you're in the office."

"Don't be daft. Of course I'm not in the office. I'm at the pool of my great friends the Zugatts, and they're just back from Bali, and they tell me there's a Balinese dance about the seven stages of happiness. Here. I'll put them on—"

"Jimmy!"

But it's too late. For the next fifteen minutes, I listen, without even mild interest, to a rambling tale of travel, featuring peanut saté and Balinese kites and bargaining for songket cloth.

I hang up, exhausted, shaking my head.

"Well, that was helpful of him," Michael says.

I give him a look that says, Boy, there's a lot of stuff they don't teach you in medical school.

"Well, it was," Michael says. "I don't see why you have to take it the wrong way."

We go grocery shopping together in the afternoon, a task we have not double-teamed since the day it ceased to be like playing house and began to *be* house. In the fruit section, Michael examines the plums as if he is feeling for a pulse. Every single thing he is doing is bugging the hell out of me.

"You're crabby," he observes, as I look disgustedly away from his fruit inspection.

"That's perceptive," I say.

"Don't be defensive," he says. "I didn't mean it as an accusation. Why are you crabby? Did you have another bad week on the book?"

I sigh. "Sometimes I think the whole thing is just crap," I tell him.

Reflexively, indulgently, Michael smiles. "I'm sure it's not crap," he says. "I'm sure it's just fine."

This is a textbook example of what I have come to think of as the reflex of marriage: the instinct to say the supportive thing, no matter what the reality. I fight this same impulse every morning, when I force myself to look before I assure Michael that his tie goes with his shirt.

"Well, how would you know if it is or isn't?" I say, and suddenly it seems clear to me, all too clear, what my problem with the book is. My problem, of course, is Michael. Michael has never read my book. Michael has never asked to read my book.

I will get to the part later about how colossally unjust this accusation is, because Michael has been, for nearly fifteen years, the very definition of the supportive spouse, offering space and time for writing and absolution for writing-related funks.

Still, I have him on a technicality, even if all I'm really doing is looking for a fight.

"You've never even read it," I say.

He pauses in the frozen-food aisle, his hand on a quart of Häagen-Dazs that he's able to eat without gaining weight, another strike against him.

"You've never asked me to," he says.

"You've never offered!" I counter—loudly enough to make him look around.

"If you're going to shout at me," he says, "could you at least wait until we get home?"

I lower my voice to a demonic hiss.

"I'm just saying," I whisper, knowing full well what my subtext is, even if—especially if—Michael does not. "How can you tell me something's fine if you don't really know if it is or isn't?"

His jaw locks. I know this jaw lock. This is the you-have-insulted-my-ability-to-understand-you-and-be-a-good-husband jaw lock. He somehow manages, presumably for the sake of the checkout girl, to keep his eyes merry enough, but his jaw is like the Tin Woodsman's, and I know now, because I have, after all, known him since we were children, I know that it will not unlock for a day or two, not until we've had the fight we're going to have.

"If you'd wanted me to read it," Michael says calmly, once we are home and unpacking the groceries, "then why couldn't you have just asked?"

"I thought it would be perfectly obvious," I say.

"So you've been sitting here, all this time, hating me for not reading your book."

No, actually, it hadn't occurred to me to use this as a strike against him until roughly half an hour ago.

But I have him on the oldest score: *He doesn't know. He doesn't know* about the camp trunks and Mom's apartment and missing the girls and the phone calls from Mom and the intrusions from T.J. *He doesn't know* how hard it is to write when you're not sure you're on the right track. *He doesn't know* how scary it is to think about the book failing, because his work never stops; there'll always be another patient, another life to save, another way to be a hero. *He doesn't know* what it's like to question the viability of your dreams.

Of course I do not tell him the most important thing he doesn't know.

But the list, as it is, is long enough. Long enough to infuriate a nice Jewish doctor whose father left his mother. Long enough to push him away and thus grant me the greater distance I need.

"Well, let me read the goddamned thing!" he finally shouts.

"No fucking way!" I shout back, and I realize that for the first time since the girls were born, I have the freedom to shout really loudly in an argument and stand up and walk out the door if I want to.

I want to.

I grab my purse and storm out, into the steamy, humid, forgiving city.

"It's cooler here," Lucas says on Tuesday as he strides into the apartment.

"Air-conditioning," I say.

"Does this mean we will no longer be punished for this sin by suffering the fires of hell?"

"Do you believe in sin?" I ask him.

It is the kind of question that I would never be able to ask

Michael, mostly because I think that by now I know everything he believes in.

"Do you think about sin a lot?" Lucas asks, putting his cigarette down on the side of a filing cabinet and removing his shirt to expose his thoroughly soft but bizarrely attractive torso.

"I think about everything a lot," I say wearily.

"You have too many clothes on," he says, and he pulls my T-shirt over my head. How does he make me feel beautiful?

I back him up toward the sofa, because the only other horizontal surface is the analyst's couch, and I am not inclined to want to let that happen.

"What everything do you think about?" Lucas asks, afterward, when, without exactly knowing I am going to do so, I take a puff of his cigarette.

"What?" I say.

"The everything you think about," Lucas says. "What is that everything?"

I look at him closely because I am fairly sure he is teasing me, but then I see in his eyes that same dark, passionate stare that I first saw at the wedding, and I turn toward him with unexpected hope.

"Smoking," I say. "I think about smoking. How much I loved smoking. Why it's so unfair that I can't smoke."

I hand back the cigarette, appalled at my lapse and, simultaneously, slightly queasy.

"I think about the kids," I say. "Writing. Alzheimer's. Money. Food. I think about eating. I think about trying to get into really good shape. I think about why some people are born thin and seem to think because of that that they've done something noble."

"Oh, I know that one," Lucas says.

"Really?"

"I'm married to that one."

"Really?"

"I think she sincerely believes that the gates of heaven are really, *really* narrow."

I laugh, feeling listened to.

"Do you ever," Lucas says, "think, Oh, to hell with the kids. I want to do what I want to do?"

"I'm here, aren't I?" I say.

"And what's this book you're writing?" he says.

"You mean the book I'm not writing?"

"Yes. What's it not about?"

I laugh.

"Happiness," I say.

He doesn't try to be witty. "Big subject," he says. "Tough subject."

"Yes."

"You must be brilliant," he says.

Must I, I wonder.

"Not brilliant enough," I say.

"Would you ever show me any of it?"

I freeze. Lucas Ross has just asked to see the work that my husband has never asked to see.

I know, at this moment, that I'm in big trouble.

What I feel, I realize later, is not only steered and controlled by Lucas but, somehow, deeply understood. Is Michael bored by discussing what lies beneath the surface of life, does he not understand it, or does he just consider it too much an extravagance to contemplate? As a doctor, of course, Michael always inhabits the world of life and death, where happiness is a luxury to experience, let alone to contemplate.

And of course I don't let myself think yet that the slightly eager, respectful look that crosses Lucas's face when I speak to him is only the look he gets when he is trying to measure how much a woman is going to adore him.

I am, however, prepared to adore him a lot.

This is what I adore about him:

I adore his questions.

I adore his hands.

I adore his language, which is unexpectedly filled with religion. *God. Heaven. Angel. Sin.*

I adore the way he touches me, as if he is a blind man, or a sculptor, trying to know me in a way that his eyes won't reveal.

I adore the way he is willing to be my playmate in this apartment, as if it is really just a clubhouse and as if we are really just kids.

Naked except for his boxers, he eats the late picnic lunch I've brought and declares that he's going to paint me.

"With what?" I ask, laughing, pretending he means now and here when I know he must mean home and later.

"With these!" he declares and brandishes the watercolors I bought for Katie and Emily.

"Oh, God," I say, and I'm laughing.

In the living room, he constructs a makeshift easel from an old reading stand, fills water glasses in the sink, and makes a palette from an old china plate. These are by far the most practical tasks I've yet seen him perform.

He passes his reflection in the window looking over the park and, almost without knowing it, sucks in his stomach and grins at himself. In his right hand is a bagel; in his left hand is a paintbrush. They are the globe and scepter of his private monarchy, which he clearly rules with equal amounts of brio and self-absorption. For Lucas, having a good day, whatever it takes, has probably always seemed the best gift he can give to anyone. To suggest that my happiness—or maybe even Marathon's—might derive from any other source but his own would be to question the entire value of the creative process in which he is so constantly, so famously, and so flamboyantly engaged.

I envy, without self-consciousness or any ambiguity, a world bathed in such an artistic light. And at this moment, I believe that Michael, however much he might love me, could never inspire me, as Lucas might, or show me by example how to make my own light bright enough.

Or maybe you can't shine that kind of light and be a wife and mother at the same time.

Or maybe that's just an excuse.

I've never, of course, been painted before.

Knowingly, Lucas pours me a glass of the white wine that T.J. has left in the fridge, and I take a long, crucial sip.

Laughing, he then positions me on the doctor's analyst couch. He has me with my back to him, reclining on my right elbow.

I take another sip of wine.

"Pretty," he tells me.

"My ass," I say.

"Yes, your ass," he says.

I am being painted by Lucas Ross.

"Lucas," I say.

"Blues and greens," Lucas says, I suppose to his palette. "Blues and greens."

"Lucas," I say again.

"Angel."

"I am not a bowl of fruit," I say.

"The hell you're not," he says and bends into his work.

16

It is better to be happy for a moment and be
burned up with beauty than to live a long time
and be bored all the while.
—*Don Marquis*

With a week to go until parents' visiting day at camp, Michael
and I simmer along in our own little wacky marital stew. It is so
odd, what many opposite and unpleasant ingredients can be added
to a marriage without seeming to affect its basic flavor. I would
never have thought I could have added adultery to the mixture and
still do the laundry and cook the dinner and say good night and
say good morning. Maybe this is one luxury of double-digit marriage. Perhaps time just absorbs the differences. A disastrous fight,
a disastrous day, maybe even a disastrous decision—just an extra
drop in the caldron, especially if you know that, in a matter of

days, you will be caught in a four-way embrace with two children you adore.

In the meantime, however, Michael is still angry that I've accused him unjustly, and I am still angry that I am married to a near-perfect being whose most irksome defects are his trust, his cereal-eating habits, and his apparent desire to stay married to me.

In a normal time, in a normal fight, I would have apologized by now. But to get any closer to Michael now means to look into a mirror that I avidly want to avoid. By a trick of scheduling, however, I am given ample opportunity to make amends: on Monday morning, I have an interview set up with a psychologist at Michael's hospital.

"Can I ride with you to work?" I ask him, trying to make it seem as if he is the one who's been acting touchy and irrational.

We ride the train together, cool and polite, beneath a subway ad for Citibank that says:

BE INDEPENDENTLY HAPPY

Phil Price, the psychologist I'm here to see, studies and treats addiction, which, I reasoned back at the hospital benefit where I'd set this thing up, must lead him into countless speculations about happiness—especially of the euphoric kind. He calls in, however, to say he'll be half an hour late. So Michael deposits me at the nurses' station on the floor where today he is teaching rounds.

I sip bad coffee and watch how his day begins.

Cryptic messages are pinned to a cluttered bulletin board:

66N DOES NOT HAVE VENODYNES.
Data is good.
Data is God.
Welcome to Lung Island.

A mini-fridge beneath the desk has a hand-scrawled sign on it that says:

Yogurt: 2 days max!

And the nurses are talking about dates and children and parents and bargains and weekend developments. It could be any workplace, any day, except that down the hall are people in pain who are waking up to another day of guessing. The blue linoleum floor is disappointingly dirty. Two abandoned Mylar get-well balloons bump along the ceiling like silver clouds.

At nine exactly, the med school students appear on the floor and cluster around my husband like groupies. They are awkward in their starched white jackets—one's is so short that it makes him look like a waiter—and they have their pockets conspicuously filled with stethoscopes, notebooks, and an embarrassing number of pens.

I see her in less than a minute. She has cropped brown hair and an upturned nose and a short skirt that shows off bionic muscles, and she is simultaneously at Michael's side and at his feet.

This is not just flirtation. I've seen flirtation. This is worship. I can spot worship from a thousand yards.

"Dr. Farber?" she asks.

"Yes, Marcie," he says.

"Dr. Farber? Did you see my chart on the stomach case?"

"Not 'the stomach case,' Marcie. That's Mrs. Kotlowitz."

"Did you see my chart on Mrs. Kotlowitz?"

"Very professional," Michael says, and off they go, down the hall, into what I imagine is Marcie's dream of rescue and safety and wooing and winning.

And here is the horrible thing:

I am jealous. But I am not jealous of Bionic Marcie for having Michael's attention. I know that Michael is not cheating on me. This is not because Michael loves me so much, or because I'm so wonderful or so worth loving. It is because Michael loves himself too much to do something that would make him so unlovable to himself. His own ego—submerged though it may be beneath the sweeping tides of his virtues—will not permit this sort of infraction.

No. What I am jealous of is Michael—for having Bionic Marcie's attention. And I am jealous because I know that when Bionic Marcie leaves, there will be another Bionic Marcie to take her place. And another. And another. An endless succession of disciples who will assess and applaud and mimic his every move.

I try to imagine how my life would feel if every time I wrote a sentence, or finished a paragraph, or set up an interview—or for that matter, every time I tied a ponytail, sliced an onion, or tore up a kitchen floor—there was someone beside me, eyes wide and wondering, ready to ask how I'd done it.

Phil Price has an interesting take on happiness. He says that people can be happy only when they are engaged in struggle.

"Our entire modern world is constructed to give us the illusion that we're not animals," he says. "But we are still animals. We need to hunt, to gather, to fight, to dominate, to procreate. These are our needs. Happiness was never part of the equation. You don't ask if a bear is happy. You don't ask if a lion is feeling good about itself. You ask if it has food, or wounds, or shelter."

On his shelf is a Spider-Man lunch box. I can't help wondering what this means.

"Addiction," Dr. Price goes on, "is usually, no matter what the sort of addiction, an effort to avoid a state of stasis. We don't like stasis. We like goals. We need needs. In the absence of needs, we create crises, and crises bring us needs."

Did my need create a crisis or did my crisis create a need?

If I were a *Mayflower* settler, my whole life would have been a crisis. That is, if I'd survived the trip. Maybe for all those hearty settlers we hear and read about, there were thousands of other women who held on like grim death to the pier. Or bitched and moaned the whole way. *I just have to do something for myself.* Would settling a wilderness count?

Dr. Price and I spend several hours in his office. I take copious notes and feel downright proud of myself for delivering what seems a plausible imitation of a writer at work on a book. This isn't so hard, I think. You come. You ask questions. You take notes. You leave.

My mood somewhat sunnier, I look for Michael on my way out, and I find him before he sees me. He is kneeling in the hallway next to a patient in a wheelchair. He is talking to her intently and cocking his head to listen. What I pick up is that she has been waiting in this hallway for an hour for some procedure, and she's uncomfortable and upset. Instinctively, almost absentmindedly, he takes her pulse while he listens to her, just another little gesture of goodness, just another touch of reassurance. He is such a good man. Fuck him.

For a moment, though, I am seized by sorrow, if not exactly by guilt.

Urgently, I want to be in love with him again. Or maybe what I mean is that I want to be alone with him again, not just alone in the bedroom at home but alone in the way that people are when they have nothing and no one else in their thoughts. It may be good to see him in this setting, I think. I just saw Lucas with a paintbrush in his hand. The least I can do is see Michael with a stethoscope in his.

I make no move closer to him, but he becomes aware of my presence—another marital magic trick.

"Excuse me," he says to the patient, and I nod to her apologetically too.

Michael comes over to stand beside me. A tiny white scab of shaving cream lies beside his right ear. I touch it, and it dissolves.

"Just thought I'd say good-bye," I tell him.

"How'd it go with Phil?"

"Fine. Good," I say. "It went well."

"He's a good guy."

"I know. Okay. Don't let me keep you."

"Something else?" he says.

"No. Anything—anything special you want for dinner tonight?" I ask him.

He smiles. "Why don't we go to a movie or something?" he asks.

"On a school night?" I say.

"It's not a school night."

"Right."

"I'll call you later," he says, and he kisses my forehead. From the corner of my eye, I see Bionic Marcie watching, and just for good measure, I plant a possessive, unambiguous kiss on Michael's lips.

"That's for your groupie," I say.

"My what?"

"Your groupie."

"What do you mean?"

"Michael."

"What groupie?" he asks, and I glance over toward Marcie.

"Don't be ridiculous," he says.

Maybe I just want to stay mad at Michael because it makes staying attracted to Lucas so much easier. But really. *What groupie?* Is Michael so wise that he sees and transcends life's lonely complexities? Or does he just not see them? How dare he be sailing so calmly and smoothly and blindly into his middle age? I am angry all over again, all the more so because I suspect that there isn't a human being on earth who would understand why I am angry. Except perhaps Lucas Ross, I think, my mind awash in shades of blue and black.

The subway home is cool and uncrowded. A woman in a halter top with flabby arms and a bruised face bends intently—even studiously—over a paperback titled *Naked in Death*. Above her head, subway ads offer carpet cleaning, legal representation, and free abortion counseling. And an ad for a skin treatment center features a giant yellow smiley face and the banner:

30 DAYS TO A HAPPIER YOU!

As long ago as 1848, a Washington boot maker named B. T. Stark printed up a flyer that said:

NOTICE TO THE LOVERS OF EASE & COMFORT.
A good fitting Boot produces ease, comfort—happiness.

In 1919, the S. S. White Dental Manufacturing Company ran a toothpaste ad in *Collier's* that was entitled "Happiness" and featured a romantic illustration of a smiling, robust maiden apparently frolicking in the woods.

Happiness is the desire of all mankind—the one goal toward which all people strive. It is the music of our days—the harmony of life. Yet how few realize that Happiness depends, largely, upon physical well being . . . and your health depends mainly upon the condition of your teeth.

In 1925, a Kotex ad claimed

Women's Happiness
Rests largely on solving
their oldest hygienic
problem *this* new way

My files at home teem with happiness ads that span decades and were employed to sell, among countless other products, Zenith radios ("Give a World of Happiness"); Union Carbide portable radios ("You can *carry* happiness with you!"); L'Aiglon Russian Leather cologne ("How to Keep Husbands Happy"); cameras ("Make somebody happy with a KODAK"); and, more recently, the New York Health & Racquet Club ("Happiness is being fit enough to get your butt kicked").

What all this happiness advertising showed was the fundamental psychological shift of the nineteenth century, from the morality of self-sacrifice to the morality of self-fulfillment. In patent medicines and women's magazines, in the advice of Freud and Spock and Betty Ford and Dr. Phil, the ethos of therapy boomed, so much so that, in the twenty-first century, success is not supposed to be a guarantee of happiness as much as happiness is supposed to be a guarantee of success.

The final, ironic corollary to this overwhelmingly self-based theory is that there is now a kind of social duty in pursuing happiness. In 1843, the very first American board game (invented by a clergyman's daughter) was called Mansion of Happiness and rewarded players' virtues by sending their pieces down a path to "the seat of happiness." By contrast, as the inventor of today's online Be Happy game puts it: "Enjoying my Happiness is the most important thing that I can do, for myself and for others."

Michael comes home too late and too tired and too sucked dry of wisdom to want to do anything as plebeian as go to a movie. It works out just as well. Online, I research the origin of the smiley face. I learn that it all began with a man named Harvey R. Ball, who was co-owner of an advertising firm in Worcester, Massachusetts. In 1963, he was paid forty-five dollars to design a button for the State Mutual Life Assurance Companies of America. The assignment was to come up with something that would boost company morale in the wake of a fractious merger. First, Ball drew a yellow circle, and then he drew a smile inside the circle. Then he tested it by turning it upside down, and, fearing that some employees might want to wear frowns instead of smiles, he drew two eyes in the circle.

By 1971, there were more than fifty million happy face buttons sold.

Ball himself never applied for a copyright and never made more than his original forty-five-dollar fee.

"He was not a money-driven guy," his son said at the time of his death. "He used to say, 'Hey, I can only eat one steak at a time.' "

Lucas, the very next day, watches me with a slightly victorious smile as I reach for one of his cigarettes, light it, inhale, lie back, and exhale.

"What?" I say.

"You like your smokes."

I laugh.

"You got that right."

"So what made you quit?"

"The surgeon general."

"You mean your husband?"

"No." I laugh again. "You know. The U.S. surgeon general? The warning on the cigarette box?"

"Never read it."

"Oh, come on."

He laughs.

"But speaking of reading," he says—and then he reminds me that I've told him he can read my book.

I swoon.

Today, he has shown up bearing a set of sheets, two new down pillows, a blanket that might be cashmere, and a box of rare Viennese chocolates, white chocolate and mocha with hazelnut centers. He says solemnly that they are the best sweets in the entire world, and that he knows of only one place—in Seattle, no less—where they're sold in this country.

I am not entirely sure that I know how to cope with a generous Lucas. My problem doesn't last long, however. I've had the bed and the wall-to-wall carpets picked up and hauled off the day before.

"What the hell were you thinking?" he asks me, hands full of bedding, furious at the sight of the vacant floor in the now empty bedroom.

"This is so sweet," I say to Lucas, deciding to ignore his anger. I stroke my cheek with the blanket. "It feels incredible," I say.

He literally tips his head up slightly, like a dog looking to be patted, then puts his arms out to receive his reward: I dive forward to kiss his lips and to circle his tongue with my own.

"I've never had sex in an empty room," Lucas says. "I might wind up liking the image."

He lowers me onto the floor and lowers himself on top of me, but even as he does so, he shifts his body and looks behind him. Perhaps, I think, he is attempting to fix the dimensions of the room in his mind. Perhaps, I think, he is trying to study the color of the walls.

The floor smells of the Murphy's Oil Soap that I used to clean it this morning. The floor is the dark wood that I remember from my childhood. Why would anyone want to cover it up with carpet? I think.

What the hell is he looking for? What does he need? I open my legs and crave him, needing the moment, the moment when all the preliminaries will be over and we'll be undressed and whatever ceremony there has to be will be over and he can just put himself inside me and I can just stop being a mouth and a mind and I can be a simple body.

"I want it," I hear myself say, and that shocks me, because I never say things like that during sex, and I haven't said it to be sexy, or to be playful, or to be bad. I've said it because I do want it, and he seems so distracted.

With me still underneath him, he tries to inch our bodies toward the far wall.

The pretext of passion fades.

"Lucas, for Christ's sake, what are you doing?"

"Watch," he says.

I can't hide my annoyance.

"Watch what?"

"Watch," he says again, and with one more glance over his shoulder, I understand that what he's been looking for is the filmy, ornate mirror that still hangs on the peeling, cracked wall, like a gray window into the past.

"Can you see it?" he asks, still attempting to adjust my line of sight to the mirror's angle.

"The mirror?"

"Us. Can you see us in the mirror? Look," he says, and with if not one motion then an impressive few, he manages to strip off my blue jeans and to pull off his shoes and socks and the khaki shorts that are dappled with his trademark paint colors of black and deep blue.

The mirror now frames his back and his buttocks and the tops of my knees. I try to look back at him, but he has put the mirror in my mind, and the kind of power I am able to see is entirely different from the kind of power I am able to feel. In short, I am given a double sensation: Lucas both in me and on me; and the double sensation astonishes me. It is simple and filthy, and it makes me come.

Later, I'll realize that it isn't just the image that had moved me. When I think about it later—as I will, given only the slightest excuse—I'll realize that what probably turned me on most was the knowledge that however close Lucas comes to me, he himself will always demand access to the outer view of what we are doing. He will never lose himself to me. He will never lose himself to any-thing, and it is the fact of this outerness that makes me keep want-ing to take him in.

I, on the other hand, can clearly lose myself to anything: to the needs of motherhood, marriage, and Mom, to T.J., to Lucas, to tiles in the kitchen and tiles in the bathroom, to finding just the right stamps to put on my letters to the girls.

I go where I think I'm needed, then say I resent the voyage.

But for now, I am lying on the hard wood floor and the soft down pillows, staring at the ceiling, and Lucas disappears and then reap-pears, grinning, and then disappears again. When he comes back, he is wearing his boxer shorts and carrying the can of white paint I bought for the bathroom and one of the sponge brushes.

"That's for the bathroom," I say.

"You can spare it," he says.

I sit up.

"Lie down," he says.

"What are you going to do?"

"Lie down," he says again.

"That's oil-based paint, Lucas," I say.

He laughs. "I know it's oil-based paint."

Still grinning, he dips the brush into the open can as if he is per-forming a sexual act, and then he carefully removes it, letting the excess paint run off.

"What are you going to do?" I ask again.

"Hush," he says.

Brandishing the brush, he kneels beside me and with a series of swift, sure strokes, he paints my outline on the floor, as if I am a murder victim and he is marking the crime scene.

"Lucas," I say. "Lucas."

But he ignores me, and I know to lie still, and then finally he says, "You can get up now. Just don't smudge the paint."

And then, without a moment's hesitation, he paints what looks like a perfect outline of himself, as if he were lying with his arms wrapped around me.

He stands back to appraise his work, then hands me the brush.

"Your turn," he says.

"What?"

"Go ahead," he says, as if it is his floor, not mine—which, given the fact that he is Lucas Ross, it actually now is.

I hand back the paintbrush, put on his T-shirt, light another cigarette, take back the brush, and for the next ten minutes or so, add lines and dots and shapes and textures outside the shapes he's painted. He watches me, as if I'm the artist, and as if what I'm making matters. Then he goes to get the other brushes and the rollers I've bought, and when he finally steps forward, his footsteps track white paint to me, and mine track footsteps back to him, so the bodies he's drawn are crisscrossed by the paths we take to each other.

Eventually, we have covered virtually the whole floor in white paint, so then—with Lucas promising me the effect will be chic and Hampton-like—we take turns rolling paint to fill in the remaining blank spots. Occasionally we get each other's feet. We laugh. We are, pretty much, kids. We paint our way out the door and stand, appraisingly, looking at a room that has been transformed from something dark and empty and ancient into something bright and full of possibilities.

In the kitchen, Lucas peels a gold wrapper ceremonially from one of the white chocolates, breaks it in two, looks at me somewhat appraisingly, then pops a half into my mouth. It is, indeed, a sublime experience.

"Gluecktorte," he says.

"Excuse me?"

"That's what they call this. Gluecktorte."

Figures. That would be translated: happycake.

17

The only joy in the world is to begin.
——*Cesare Pavese*

It has become so tempting to want to tell T.J. For one thing, it's annoyingly difficult to talk to her every morning and pretend that there's nothing really new. My "Fine" is simply not an honest or adequate answer to her "How are you?" And then there's the guilty but undeniable pride I feel, the impulse to boast and gloat and, yes, even to enjoy watching her rethink (however briefly) our relative female assets. T.J. is always having men fall at her feet, and I am never having men fall (or even stumble) at my feet, and she knows this. So on Wednesday morning, when she tells me about how her new Pilates instructor admired the muscle tone in her thighs, and I hear that mixture of coyness and superiority in her voice, it's all

I can do to keep from shouting "Guess who admires the muscle tone in *my* thighs? Yes, *my* thighs?"

Happiness, I suppose, is sometimes hard to separate from base, ignoble, loathsome, and delicious spite.

In our morning phone call, she also tells me about a new stress-relieving gadget that Ethan has found for her. It is called the Lightscape Relaxation System®, and he bought it for her at Sharper Image (online, of course). According to T.J., this is a gadget that comes with special glasses and headphones, and when you put them on, you get to see a miniature light show and hear various soothing sounds like oceans and whispering pines.

"And what's this supposed to do for you?" I ask.

"Relieve my stress."

"Sex would do that too," I say merrily.

And yes, I am merry this morning. Not just happy, but merry, and when I hang up with T.J. and I sit down to work, I am astonished to discover that, contrary to all my expectations, it seems I can write again.

Sometimes, writing feels like an almost tangible endeavor. Words are bricks. Ideas are mortar. Paragraphs are tall, fine walls. And all the little niceties (like how words are bricks and ideas are mortar and paragraphs are tall, fine walls) are the decorative motifs that can make the difference between a structure you remember and one you forget.

I don't know why, or how, or how long this will last, but when I sit down to work this afternoon, the ideas that have been shuffling around my brain all summer like sodden, drunken freshmen suddenly sit up, lean forward, and listen.

I work at my aging laptop in my slightly peeling kitchen, and the sink is filled with coffee cups and breakfast plates, and there is a spatter of spaghetti sauce on the backsplash behind the stove, and now I don't care. I don't care. Lucas Ross and I are having sex together. Lucas Ross and I are painting floors together. Lucas Ross wants to see what I've written, and so I want to write something that will be worthy of his wish.

Here is my revelation, which comes just a few minutes after four o'clock, nearly two years into writing this book: The problem is the outline. I have organized the book chronologically. The history of happiness, beginning with Aristotle and ending with Oprah. But realistically, the different definitions of happiness all have their *own* histories. How can I take the concept of *pleasure,* for example, and confine it to a chapter on Epicurus? Epicurus was very clear on the point that pleasure is the goal of all human actions. He used a human infant's avoidance of pain and seeking of pleasure as proof that the human instinct is toward happiness. He argued also that even the most seemingly altruistic gestures are in themselves a pursuit of pleasure (a point I wholeheartedly agree with in this anti-Michael state of mind). But how can I separate this from my later discussion of Timothy Leary and the uses of LSD? I shouldn't have a chapter about Epicurus, or even about the ancient Greeks, I think, but a chapter about pleasure.

So I take out an actual notebook—this is too much fun not to write by hand—and I make the list I've been wanting to make all along, without exactly knowing it. My list goes by theme:

Pleasure
Freedom
Goodness
Beauty
Love
Genetics
Faith
Health

And I love this list so much that I actually rewrite it, on a clean page, in my best handwriting, as if I am making some gesture of gratitude, or allegiance. And quickly, before I can change my mind or allow it to have any other thoughts at all, I move my computer's cursor to File and then New, and on a fresh blank screen that doesn't know what's about to hit it, I type the words

What if happiness is pleasure?

In the fourth century before Christ, when Aristotle's definition of happiness was still lingering in the Aegean air, a philosopher named Epicurus stepped forward to declare that Aristotle had been wrong. Happiness had nothing to do with goodness. Happiness had everything to do with pleasure or, rather, with the avoidance of pain. Epicurus looked around and decided that the greatest obstacle to man's happiness was anxiety. And so he came up with a four-point plan for how people could enjoy the happiness that they naturally wanted to enjoy: "Don't fear god, don't worry about death, what's good is easy to get, and what's terrible is easy to endure."

A vaguely familiar lyric pops into my head, something left over from a presidential campaign. *Don't worry. Be happy.* So I go online, and I search for these words, and I find the song lyrics, floating on a screen filled with yellow happy faces. Then I switch back to my own screen and type:

In a nutshell, Epicurus's philosophy would be summed up two millennia later in the immortal words of the songwriter Bobby McFerrin:

Here's a little song I wrote
You might want to sing it note for note

Don't worry, be happy.
In every life we have some trouble
When you worry you make it double
Don't worry, be happy.
Don't worry, be happy now.

Ain't got no place to lay your head
Somebody came and took your bed
Don't worry, be happy.
The landlord say your rent is late
He may have to litigate
Don't worry, be happy.

And now, excited and, yes, happy, I sit for a moment, pondering, actually pondering, this Epicurean-McFerrinean construct, and I think: Okay, why *not* smoke, why *not* have nonmarital sex, why *not*—while I'm at it—have a slice of cheesecake, a brownie, another Gluecktorte? Why not sit out in Riverside Park and tilt my head back to feel the sun on my face instead of reading the book I've supposedly gone outside to read?

In the view of the mythology expert Joseph Campbell—made famous in a two-thousand-part PBS series with Bill Moyers—the goal of the well-lived life is to "follow your bliss," to pursue those aspects of living that enable you to partake in the experience of *being alive.*

In Lucas's presence, I have felt the unmistakably rhythmic pulse of being alive.

So why *not* seek those moments, the light on the water? Isn't it even an American right?

In October of 2003, the President's Council on Bioethics produced a report titled *Beyond Therapy: Biotechnology and the Pursuit of Happiness.* In it, the authors examined the implications of biotechnology in relation to human individuality and happiness and wrote that "according to the Declaration of Independence, the right to pursue happiness is one of the unalienable rights that belong equally to all human beings."

But Thomas Jefferson almost certainly did not mean what we think he meant when he added "the pursuit of happiness" to his short list of Americans' unalienable rights. What *happiness* meant in the context of the Declaration of Independence—in the usually forgotten context of one very long sentence asserting the right to rebel—remains the source of considerable debate among scholars. But the general feeling seems to be that *happiness* meant something much more akin to *material goods, physical security,* and even *a peaceful society* than it did to the emotional state with which we associate the word today.

John Locke, in his 1690 *Second Treatise on Civil Government,* wrote famously of man's rights to "life, liberty, and property." And so a lot of people think Jefferson's phrase is a direct and telling edit of that one. But possibly more relevant and certainly more recent at the time of Jefferson's writing was the example of his friend George Mason, who in a draft of the Virginia Declaration of Rights wrote: "All men are born equally free and independent, and have certain inherent natural rights . . . among which are the enjoyment of life and liberty, with the means of acquiring and possessing property, and pursuing and obtaining happiness and safety." As Robert Darnton writes in *George Washington's False Teeth:* "Mason's wording runs exactly parallel to the famous phrase that Jefferson wrote in the Declaration of Independence a few weeks later. It suggests that happiness is not opposed to property but is an extension of it."

In short: Thomas Jefferson can't really help you if what you're looking for is a way to justify having a fifth shot of vodka, or taking a three-hour lunch, or abandoning your family so you can finally see Maui. Or having an affair.

❋

Eat, drink, and be merry?

Smoke, screw, and be giddy?

For tomorrow we die.

Of course, the only true enemy of this form of happiness is *consequence*. The inevitable *then* after the *if*.

If you smoke, then you will get cancer.

If you eat, then you will get fat.

If you lie, then you will be found out. Divorced. Alone.

But can we ever really know what will make us happy and what will not?

And what if none of the bad things happen?

What if you're one of those people who lives to be a hundred, and when the *Today* show comes to interview you and ask you what your secret is, you say you smoked, ate, and fondled whatever the hell you wanted to?

Or what if you do indeed die tomorrow? What if, say, you're in the middle of pitching a new campaign for a glow-in-the-dark lipstick, and an air-conditioning duct happens to cave in on your head? Wouldn't you feel like a schmuck if "I'm not eating carbs" were among your last words?

It wasn't any wise old general who said "Eat drink and be merry, for tomorrow we die." It was the author of Ecclesiastes, who also said there was a time to lose and a time to get.

We all know we will die tomorrow. We just don't know if tonight is going to last a night or a lifetime.

Wouldn't it be lovely if someone could invent a new form of amnesia: a way of forgetting what's in the future instead of what's in the past?

Absentmindedly, I click back on the Internet screen, and suddenly, the be-boppy music of McFerrin's song fills my kitchen:

Ain't got no cash, ain't got no style
Ain't got no gal to make you smile
Don't worry, be happy.

And I think:

Going to regret having this affair
But it's helping me write my book again so I don't care
Don't worry, be happy.

18

> Ask yourself whether you are happy,
> and you cease to be so.
> —*John Stuart Mill*

*L*et's talk about car happiness. Automobile-driving, open-road happiness. Tunes-on-the-radio, wind-in-the-hair happiness. In pre–Pearl Harbor 1941, Dodge produced a sales booklet for its newest model that featured a map on the cover with a street sign labeled PLEASURE AHEAD and a town called Happiness Hollow (a contradiction in terms if ever I've seen one). The ad said:

TO REAL HAPPINESS IN 1941

So let's talk about being behind the wheel of a car. I think this is freedom, pushing independence. I think this is the illusion of flight. It is the one situation I know of in life where, for whole hours at a time, I can feel completely free of my own body.

I ask Michael if I can take the first shift on our drive up to camp on Saturday, and he nods knowingly, tolerating my desire to feel free, and he climbs into the passenger side of our neglected black Volvo wagon.

My father taught me to drive. He also taught me how to check the oil, check the water, change a flat, and jump-start a battery. "I don't want you to grow up to be one of *those* girls," he would say.

I always think of my father when I'm behind the wheel of a car, and this morning I let myself wonder what my life would have been like if he hadn't died. Would I have married Michael if I hadn't felt such a grave, grim need to be safe?

We set out at 9:00 A.M. to whir down the summer highway, following the yellow lines as if our car is connecting the dots of some vast, still-unspecified drawing. And it may be that an entire hour goes by before either of us says a word. And then, just as we are getting onto the Taconic Parkway, he says:

"I read it."

I am in the middle of reliving the mirror scene with Lucas in my head, and so it takes me a moment to realize that Michael is speaking. He repeats himself.

"I read it, Sally. I thought it was wonderful. Fascinating. I don't see the problem."

"What part did you read?" I ask.

"All of it. I mean, whatever was in the binder on your desk."

"When?"

"What?"

"When did you read it?"

"The other night," he says. "When you were late coming home from shopping."

I'd told him I was shopping. What I was really doing was using a brutal combination of steel wool and turpentine to get the white paint off the soles of my feet.

I am silent.

"I thought it was wonderful," he says.

"You did?"

"I really did. But you had me fooled. I was terrified. I really was starting to think from what you said that it was going to be terrible."

"It *was* terrible," I say, fully intending to tell him how I've figured out a new approach. But Michael has other ideas.

"Pull over," he says.

I check the speedometer, the rearview mirror, the shoulder.

"Why?"

"I want to talk to you," he says.

"I want to get there," I say.

"Pull over," he says again, furious, commanding.

And so I do, ending my escape, my free fall, my flight, in a humid patch of sharp, tall grass and dandelion weeds.

Flies and yellow jackets circle the discarded bags and sandwich wrappers at our feet. It is only ten o'clock, but I am already tired and hungry. I don't want to have the fight that Michael is poised to have. I am still lying on the wood floor of an empty room that smells of Murphy's Oil Soap. I am still staring at the white contour of my body, where it fell.

"I'm sorry," I say, intending to go through the motions, but at the sight of the sadness and rage in Michael's eyes, I feel unexpectedly sincere.

"Why are you doing this?" Michael asks, as if feelings are choices—which, not incidentally, some researchers think they can be.

"Why am I doing what?"

"Why are you acting as if I'm the enemy? All summer long it's seemed like you've been trying to make me the bad guy. Why?"

"I don't know," I say, and I am crushingly contrite. "I'm sorry," I say again. "You haven't done anything wrong. It's just—"

"Do you think maybe it's time you go back on the Zoloft?" he asks me.

This question normally enrages me, every bit as much as "Are you getting your period?" used to. And they mean the same thing, which is: *Your feelings don't exist. They are just a tenuous bridge of chemical components that can collapse at any time.* But today Michael's question seems entirely appropriate.

I first started taking Zoloft when I quit smoking, a process that took as much stamina as labor—and probably five times as much strength.

As I am pondering Michael's question, another car pulls up in the long grass ahead of us. Another couple steps out, looking troubled and angry, already engaged in hot dialogue.

I have a sudden, rogue thought that this shoulder of the highway is for fighting couples only. I can imagine a new universal rest-stop sign. In addition to the little yellow squares decorated by fork and knife, phone, gas pump, and bed, I envision two lollipop people with cartoon curse symbols floating above their heads.

Naturally, I laugh.

Naturally, this infuriates Michael.

"There's nothing funny about this," he says.

"No," I say. "Look. Look over there. At them."

He turns around to see this other couple, and because Michael and I have known each other our whole lives, and perhaps because he is the one true love in my life, he turns back to me, laughing, and says, "Marital Conflict Stop."

I hug him impulsively, and then he says, "Is this what they mean by a shoulder to cry on?" and I laugh even harder, really laugh, and I love that I don't have to explain what is funny about the other fighting couple. Even if there are some things he may not understand, this is clearly not one of them. And in this moment, I want to be part of Michael again, want never to have kissed, let alone made love to, let alone painted a floor with another man. I want to tell Michael everything and know that the loving thing is to tell him nothing.

The stranger I've been living with for all these weeks vanishes, and standing before me in the humid, disgusting, fly-buzzing heat is the person I love the most in the world.

We arrive in Lee, Massachusetts, at exactly 11:30. We find the camp easily but are not allowed to be there before noon. So we walk slowly through the stifling town, saying we're looking for coffee but really just killing time. I am holding Michael's hand, despite both his and my own slightly sweaty palms. I am feeling a bit like Jimmy Stewart at the end of *It's a Wonderful Life*.

We say nothing until, on a street corner, I stop and put my arms around him and start to cry.

"It's okay, sweetheart," he tells me, and his hands, which I know have taken so many pulses, and given so many injections, and patted so many shoulders, find their way to the sides of my face. He holds my face in his hands, masterfully, and kisses me emphatically, and says: "That's enough of that now."

Half an hour later, we are lined up by the gates at the foot of the campus along with several hundred yearning parents, hearts on fire with anticipation. At the top of the hill, like a pack of seething game-show contestants, our children stand in front of their bunks, awaiting the signal to run down and find us.

Over a distant, vaguely militaristic loudspeaker, a gong sounds, and in a moment all the children come charging down the hill, ponytails flying, braces catching the sunlight, arms churning the air.

I know I should be looking for both children at once, but I am looking for the one who I know will be looking harder for me. And indeed, excitement, or perhaps desperation, compels Emily into her greatest athletic feat of all time. She has seen us from the top of the hill and is in the very first row of campers, working her legs as hard as she can, and there is a smile pushing her cheeks up around her eyebrows, and she is tan, and her legs are longer, and she looks so beautiful, a brown berry with legs. Over our embrace, and her perfume of insect repellent and slightly chlorinated hair, I see Katie, slowing down slightly to find us, which she does, and I shift Emily onto my right arm and open my left arm to Katie.

Michael stands by patiently. Ten years of fatherhood have taught him that motherhood means you get the first hugs. But when it is his turn, the girls manage to tumble him onto the grass, laughing. I am awed, to the point of crying, by the sight of the three of them.

In the first hour, every question we ask is answered carelessly with the word *great*. How's the weather? How's your bunk? How's your swim teacher? How's your swimming? What's it like when it rains here?

As a foursome, we visit first Katie's, then Emily's bunk, and in each place we unload the cookies and candy and gum that we have been directed by Katie to bring. I have kept our contributions to the food pile extremely minimal. A tin each of home-baked cookies. A pack each of chewing gum. As I'd anticipated, the food scene has a feeling of Halloween excess, and the bunks, which upon first entry were ready-for-inspection neat, are stunningly, instantly, a confetti assortment of candy wrappers, jump-rope-length strings of licorice, twelve-packs of Cherry Coke, and unopened bags of sunflower seeds. There is a frenzy of unwrapping and swapping and eating and hugging and introductions and awkward silences, and then all the mothers, as if following some sinister ultrasonic signal, start to try to tidy things up.

Katie is the first to rebel.

"Stop, Mom!" she says.

"But just the garbage—" I begin.

"Mom."

"Where's the trash can?" I say.

"We'll do it at the end!" she nearly shouts.

And I realize I'm messing with her ritual. And this makes it clear: I want, but don't have, any real job here. And then I remember, with something like hope, that I have this job—it's called writing a book—and it's waiting for me at home.

We break into teams to watch their classes. I start out with Katie, because she wants me to see her archery class.

So we troop off into the woods, a dozen awkward-looking parents trailing after two counselors and our newly woodsy city daughters. The counselors look about twenty and obviously think we're idiots. The girls are less blasé, but still, they will not be mommed around.

And so, having conquered the impulse to clean their bunks, we now have to tame the ancient instinct to warn them that their bows and arrows could put somebody's eye out.

I'm with Emily for the second period, and Michael's with Katie— and along with the already weary-looking parents, I sit in the bleachers poolside, watching a swimming class, which is a bit like watching a swimming pool, except that occasionally a hopeful tan face will bob up from the water and say something to me that I can't quite hear.

The girls swim. They do racing turns. They float. They stand by the pool, their bodies a bizarre range from little-girl pudgy to nearly female. They dive. They do that camp thing of holding their noses and dipping their heads back to slick down their hair. I smile at Emily and wonder when she will start to look like one of the nearly female types, and I shudder, imagining the inevitable changes, for which I feel every bit as unready as she. I will myself to think of Epicurus and/or Bobby McFerrin. Future Amnesia, I think. *You will not fear the future,* and indeed, at this moment, the present seems more compelling. For the moment, my daughter seems at ease and confident, and hey: in the water, she floats.

✳

We sneak the girls off to Friendly's for lunch. Technically, we are not allowed to take Katie off campus, only Emily. The younger girls, for some reason, are not trusted out in the world. But I am in a reckless, giddy mood. I played jacks with both girls on the floor of Emily's cabin, the jangle of the jacks and the thud of the ball and the cutesy terminology bringing me back to my childhood, and fast.

What if the secret of happiness turns out to be getting to tensies in one turn?

Friendly's is jammed with dozens of different versions of us. We opt for takeout from the back window. The line there is long as well, but I have played jacks and so I am suddenly a patient, generous, loving person, and I motion the kids and Michael onto the freshly mown grass, and I designate myself the food gatherer.

I know from my book that a couple of researchers in the Netherlands have developed a study based on something called the Groningen Enjoyment Questionnaire. The idea of the study was to find a universal way in which people could describe how much they enjoyed different physical activities that they did in their leisure time. I am trying to decide whether jacks would qualify as a physical activity.

I smile at the thought and catch my reflection in the glass window of the take-out booth. For once, I don't mind the way that I look. I look like a just-about-middle-aged mom, on a visit to see her not-quite-teenaged girls, and the place and the age that I am right now do not trouble me somehow. I am actually smiling. I've caught myself smiling. My daughters and husband are waiting for me.

"Sally!" I hear a sugary voice say. And amazingly, I don't even mind the fact that when I turn around I meet, head-on, the specter of Abbie Prynn. Yes, she is standing there wearing madras shorts and a sleeveless button-down shirt that I might have fit into when I was fourteen, and yes, she has not a single hair out of place, and yes, Celia—across whose chest one of Abbie's skinny arms is draped, snakelike—is absolutely knockout gorgeous. But I just played jacks, and my daughters and husband are waiting for me, and at home, I'm actually writing a book.

"Tom couldn't come," Abbie announces before I can say anything, and I experience one of those rare moments of perspective, in which I realize that the women I'm usually most afraid of being judged by are every bit as scared of being judged themselves.

Abbie Prynn, with all her blond, cool certainty, suddenly becomes a skinny girl doing her best to keep things going while the man in her life has left her stranded and known that she would come through.

"I'm sure he would have loved to," I say, instantly magnanimous. "I'm sure he would have loved to see your camp, and you, Celia," I say to Celia, who ends the Kodak moment by shrugging and picking a scab.

"Celia!" Abbie says, and I feel so sorry for her at this moment that I honestly want to embrace her.

"You're welcome to join us," I say, before I know that I've really said it.

But a wiser, or at least a cooler, head prevails, and once the Prynns' name is called, they gather their take-out food and leave.

Forty minutes later, Michael is lying with his head on my canvas bag, and I am lying with my head on his chest, and Emily is lying with her head on my chest, and Katie is lying with her head on Emily's chest. We probably look like a set of human dominoes, and I laugh at the thought, sending a chain reaction of laughter down to the youngest domino and back again, and then I sigh, looking up at the summer leaves, which shift lazily and fan us in the still, sweet July heat. If happiness is this easy, how can it also be so impossibly hard?

*

A few years ago, PBS sponsored a photo contest in which it asked participants to illustrate the phrase "the pursuit of happiness." Perhaps public television viewers—or for that matter, judges—are a special breed, not particularly materialistic in their responses. But in fact, the vast majority of the winning photographs showed smiling family members. There were no images of Manolo Blahnik shoes, stacks of gold coins, naked women, or, come to think of it, naked artists. There were photographs of sleeping children, running children, playing children, newborn children. Whatever happiness was, the results of the contest seemed to suggest, its pursuit was clearly taking place inside, not outside, the family.

It is after Arts and Crafts, when I am trying to pick the bits of glitter out of Emily's hair, that she first starts to look sad.

Around us, in the corridor of the activities center, I notice that girls have splintered off somewhat from their parents and are doing two-by-two girl things with each other. Jokes. Hair. Cat's cradle. Gross-out stuff. Out on the lawn in front, I can see Celia Prynn literally prancing as she performs some sort of song.

"Do you ever play with Celia?" I ask Emily, as gently as I can, and in one hot second, the tears come to her eyes, and it is all over.

"What?" I say, feeling utterly betrayed and, unforgivably, looking around to see who will witness this breakdown.

It takes Emily a moment to collect herself, and around us, twittering girls and their mothers look away, pretending not to hear.

"What?" I whisper now.

Emily shakes her head fiercely, indicating that she has at least some pride.

So we wait while the other girls rush off to their next activities, and I ask the counselor if I can talk to Emily myself a minute, and she says fine, it's just Nature class, and Emily and I walk, holding hands, toward the woods that encircle the camp.

"Oh, Mommy," she says, and her arms clutch my waist. Her head is now up to my chest, which seems impossible, but it must have been true a month ago, too, and something dissolves in me, because this physical contact is like nothing else in the world. It is not marital, not adulterous, not anything like that. The closest thing I know to it is the feeling of clean sheets beneath me and a heavy quilt on top with, say, a sunset to look at, and a cold breeze coming in through a window. She fits against my body. She is some lost other part of me.

When she stops crying, I comb her bangs with my fingers, and wait.

What comes forth is a tale of woe, of teasing, torture, loneliness. It turns out that the Eenies—Luceeny, Tineeny—have been running riot. They are the camp enforcers, demanding obeisance from all inmates, taking bribes of candy and gum in exchange for inclusion in nightly rituals like spooky storytelling, boyfriend confessionals (they're ten!), and a succession of jokes and jingles pertaining to every digestive function. If they deign to ask you, and if you pony up your goodies, you can be an Eeny, but even then there's a hierarchy. The very top Eenies meet daily after lunch and before nap to decide what the nightly agenda will be.

Needless to say, Emily is not now nor has she ever been an Eeny.

But more than that, she has never been asked to be an Eeny.

And—bottom line, here—she's had enough.

She wants to come home.

All this comes spilling out, relatively coherently, as we sit in the shade of a particularly beautiful elm tree. Emily's tanned face grows somewhat pale with the telling, and as I listen to her I notice that a huge, I mean huge, I mean almost comically huge, spider is nestled on the tree bark about a foot above her head, and I make another in a long series of Emily calculations: Do I leave the spider in place and risk the unpleasantness of spider bite or spider landing, or do I sweep the thing away and risk the specter of lasting spider anxiety? I decide to leave the spider in place.

"I've tried all summer long, Mommy," Emily says, and I believe her. "I mean, every single day, I've tried. I mean it. I've been so nice to them! I always offer to share stuff, and I gave Luceeny—I mean Lucy—I gave her my last hair elastic. And I always laugh at all their stupid jokes. I mean, Mom, would you want to spend every lunchtime hearing these totally gross jokes?"

"No, I wouldn't," I admit.

The spider begins, slowly, to crawl closer to Emily's head.

"I hate gross jokes!" my daughter shouts, and her words seem to echo in the woods, words uttered with far more confidence than I suspect she's shown all summer.

"There's only four more weeks," I say, trying to be helpful.

"*Only!*"

"Well, all right. Let's put it this way. There's four more weeks."

Tears fill her eyes and then spill out. Her mouth works back and forth, like a marionette's, as she struggles not to sob.

"Please, Mommy," she finally says in a whisper.

"Oh, sweetheart," I tell her. I open my arms, and as she leans forward, I flick the spider off the tree.

In retrospect, the problem is that I don't have enough time to sort it all out, let alone to consult with Michael and find out what he thinks.

I am so besotted by the prospect of reclaiming my marriage that to reclaim my daughter also seems the ideal activity for this hot July afternoon.

What I mean to say to her, rocking her in my arms, is simply "It's okay, it's okay, it's okay." But somehow that changes to "Okay, okay, okay," which she hears—and all right, I probably mean it, anyway—as "It's okay. You can come home."

"Do you think," my former shrink asked me once, "that it's your responsibility to make your children happy?"

"Of course," I answered, before I realized it was a trick question.

"No, seriously," she answered back.

Happy, I thought at the time. Isn't that the whole idea?

"How can you not want your child to be happy?" I asked.

And indeed, if you ask any of the parents in our circle—from T.J. to Abbie Prynn and back again—what they want their children to be when they grow up, *happy* is the word you are most apt to hear. In fact that's even become the politically correct response these days, far more common and infinitely more acceptable than any number of answers you might hear if the parents were force-fed truth serum: answers like *rich* or *successful* or *pretty* or even *bound for the Ivy League.* Michael and I have often discussed this, have often talked about the relative merits of other words, words such as *strong, independent,* and *generous,* and also that most out-of-date word *nice.* Even before I was researching happiness, I knew—and occasionally managed to live by—Mark Twain's famous statement: "The best way to cheer yourself up is to try to cheer somebody else up."

Somehow, though, in the sweep and embrace of this moment, I have forgotten that there might be something more important than Emily's being happy.

Michael, of course, has not forgotten. He is so adamant about the benefits of independence and separation that I know, immediately and furiously, that he is not only talking about Emily but talking about me too. And I know, immediately and furiously, that I'm not just wrong to want her back home but in fact colossally wrong.

His rightness, though, makes me fight back, out of shame far more than conviction.

"How can you not care?" I ask him.

"How can you possibly say I don't care?"

I can hear the echo of our lunchtime laughter fading into the distance like an evening song.

I watch Emily dissecting beetles and moths and butterflies during Nature. Then I tell her she can't come home with us. I realize by her reaction that I believed she was coming home more than she did.

"I'm sorry," I say as we walk back to her cabin to meet Michael and Katie for the last hour. I am holding Emily's hand, and she squeezes it, hard, and now it is my turn to work my jaw back and forth, trying not to cry.

It turns out that they have one particularly hideous ritual at this camp. The gong sounds, and the campers and parents are told over the loudspeaker that it's time to go now, and that the campers are not allowed to walk their parents to the cars. Hugs and kisses ensue, and things are relatively manageable until a slightly warped tape plays:

The party's over,
It's time to call it a day . . .

Our girls are no better or worse off than most. Even Emily seems to be more exhausted than anything else, and so I say good-bye to them and turn away as quickly as I can. I nearly run back down the hill, not wanting to draw out the torture for them or for me.

I am blinded by tears, the leave-taking, and I have to get back to the car, to the road, to the now-twilit and ever-so-sad illusion of one last flight.

Does Michael know how much I want to hold on? To him and to us and to the moment on the grass? Does he know that, despite this wanting, I can already feel my grasp slipping again, as we ride along in the sinking darkness into our middle age?

19

Be happy while you're living,
for you're a long time dead.
—*Scottish proverb*

It should be over with Lucas. I should be thanking him for the inspiration, the paint job, the sex, and the chocolates and sending him on his brilliant way. But I don't. On the last Tuesday in July, I wait for him at Mom's apartment with the noblest of intentions, but then he is five minutes late, then ten, then fifteen. And by the time he rings the doorbell and I open the door to find his slightly sweaty, slightly annoyed, ever deep and disheveled look, I am totally gone.

"Now," he says to me fifteen minutes later.

He is not giving me a direction or a command. He is giving me a warning.

"Now," he says again, almost shouts, and indeed, right then, he comes—in a rush of emphatic speed, and with the accompaniment of extremely loud and vivid religious imagery.

He collapses, proud and sweaty, on top of me, and breathes noisily, for emphasis. Eventually, he slides off me to lie by my side.

His astonishing hands, with their long, cool, perfectly symmetrical fingers, reach, unexpectedly, to stroke my hair.

I eye him warily, sexily, possessively. His stroking becomes a tug. He tugs at my hair, and our eyes meet, and for a split second, our usual flashing flirtation steadies itself into something more like honest assessment. We lie, two virtual strangers who are naked and sweaty and passionate, and for this moment we meet each other's eyes for the first time, allowing a peek at some true nakedness. No playfulness dancing in there just now. No lurid, lecherous promises. Just—his eyes. And not even the artist's eyes, for what they can see. But the man's eyes, for what they can hold. Fleetingly, I permit myself to wonder: Is it possible? I know he would inspire me. Understand me. Believe me.

"What am I going to do with you?" he says, almost peevishly.

I try not to let my eyes betray my leaping, foolish heart.

"Didn't you just do it?" I say.

"Not *to* you, Sally. *With* you," he says.

But then he stands up, scratches his ass, and walks to the kitchen, where he finds his precious Gluecktortes exactly where he has left them, shimmering in the fridge.

"What's on your mind?" he asks me as he leads the way back to the living room and peels the gold foil from the chocolates with the same expression I usually see when he removes my clothes.

"On my mind?" I ask.

"Yep," he says.

What's on my mind is what he has just asked: What is he going to do with me? What, please, are the options? But I can't ask him this, at least not now, so instead I say: "What do you think about when you work?"

"Oh," he says, sighing. "That," he says. He pops the entire chocolate into his mouth. He takes his glass of white wine from the floor beside the doctor's couch. He sips and looks down pensively.

"Or let me guess," I say. "You probably don't like to talk about your work."

"Oh, no, I love to talk about my work," he says.

"You do?"

"Don't you?"

"What makes you think my work is anything even remotely like your work?" I ask.

"Well, you're a writer, aren't you?"

"Yes."

"Well, writers are artists," he says generously.

"Not all writers are artists," I say.

"Well, you are," he answers.

"You're only saying that because you're having sex with me."

Lucas considers this and takes another sip of wine. "True," he says.

I laugh.

"Do you ever have writer's block?" I ask him. "I mean, whatever the equivalent is—painter's block?"

"No."

"Never?"

"Never."

"Isn't art supposed to be hard?" I ask him.

"Look, my mother always told me my shit was beautiful," he says.

I laugh.

"I am not being metaphorical," he says. "I mean, literally. My mother literally told me that my shit was beautiful."

"Literally?"

"Literally."

I try, for a moment, to imagine that. First his mother. Then mine. The image is impossible. The closest my mother ever got to praise was to ask why I thought I needed it.

"My mother never told me that sort of thing," I say to Lucas.

"It shows," he says.

"It does?"

Abruptly, he starts to pull on his clothes. I don't have to wonder why. The conversation has simply slipped away from him, slipped out of the realm of sex and into the realm of caring. This isn't what he had in mind. But I can't quite let him go yet. It is almost as if, having discovered the path back to Michael this weekend, I now have the freedom to stand and linger at the crossroads—and maybe even venture further down the path I know less well.

I am hit by a breathtaking, reckless thought: What if the person Lucas is underneath the sex and the cigarettes and the weird, retro sense of freedom is the man I'm supposed to be with? Maybe even, my roadside revelations about Michael notwithstanding, the man I was supposed to be with all along?

"You said you wanted to read my book," I say, ashamed of myself the minute I hear my own words.

"I did?" he asks. There is a stain on his black T-shirt, but I decide not to tell him this. Let Marathon worry about his stains.

"Yes," I say. "You asked me if you could read it."

"Oh. Well. Right. Do you want me to read it?"

I glance down, hoping he'll think I'm looking for my socks.

"If you want to," I finally say and look up, and he smiles at me as if he is glancing at some rare zoo animal, caged and vaguely exotic.

"Good, then," he says. "I'll look forward to it. See you next week," he says. "I've got to run, now. See you."

And with a chaste, profoundly patronizing kiss to my forehead, he removes himself from the net of my need: the need to be kissed both chastely and not; the need to be told I'm an artist and told that I don't have to be an artist; the need to be screwed and then listened to; the need to be tortured and soothed.

❅

It takes me till at least eight that evening to remember that I'd been planning to end it with him.

"How's it coming?" my mother asks me on the phone that night.

"It's coming," I say.

"Well, give me an update, will you?"

So I tell her: about the pulled-up carpet, the newly painted white floor, the boxes of books being shipped out, the garbage bins filled with cracked china. I tell her about the doctor's file cabinets and the files, which I've not yet been able to toss, because how can you just throw out an entire life's work?

"Well, she didn't have any family," Mom says.

"I *know* that, Mom."

"It's not like anyone's ever going to *need* that stuff."

"I *know,* Mom, but it's— I don't know. Wouldn't you hate it if all your letters and papers and things are just thrown out when you die?"

"I'll be dead."

"But—"

"You're just like your father," she says—a rare reference that makes me perk up.

"What do you mean?"

"He liked saving *everything*. He had all these things from his parents, you know, and from that brother of his who died. And, I don't know, just *things*. From our honeymoon, even. Pebbles. Acorns. So much junk."

"What did you do with it?" I ask gently.

"Who knows? I couldn't keep it *all*."

"You could have given it to me."

"You were in college."

"What's that got to do with it?"

"Who ever saw you then?"

I take a deep breath. With the portable phone, I have been pacing the apartment, and now I find myself in the girls' darkened bedroom.

"Mom," I say. "Let's change the subject."

I sit in the old rocking chair, the one I logged so many miles in when the girls were babies. I should give it away, already, and replace it with something more comfortable. Is there any chance, after all, that I will have another child?

"Well, Janet McGoogan called me," Mom says. "She wants to be able to list the apartment by the Labor Day, when everyone comes back from the Hamptons."

"Labor Day, Mom. Not the Labor Day."

"When everyone comes back," she repeats. "That's only a month away, you know."

I feel unexpectedly panicked that the summer is slipping away.

Time flies when you're having sex.

"I should be done by Labor Day," I say.

"I would have thought you'd be done by now."

I think: Sorry, Mom, I've been slowed down somewhat by a tempestuous affair with an irresistible, world-famous artist who may be the love of my life.

I say: "Sorry, Mom."

"Well, don't disappoint me," she says cheerily, then signs off to go spread her special brand of joy elsewhere.

Could she ever have felt about me what I feel about my girls? And oh, how deeply I hope my girls never feel about me what I feel about her.

On Thursday, T.J. calls me from the road. She is on her cell phone, as usual, but the static is worse than ever.

"Where the hell are you?" I all but shout.

"What?"

"Where the hell are you?"

"Atlanta," she says.

"Why?"

"Sales conference."

"How's it going?"

"Fine."

Again, I battle the impulse to tell her what's going on. Would she really tell Marathon? And would it make a difference? Is Marathon one of those women who knows all and accepts all, or is she the type who would leave Lucas if she knew what he's been doing? And as my mother would doubtless say, what is that to me?

"What's going on with you?" I ask T.J.

"Do you think Ethan's having an affair?" she asks.

"Ethan?"

"I'm down here with Marathon," she says, "and she was telling me the other night about how Lucas had this affair a few years ago, and I just started wondering."

"Wondering what?" I ask, suddenly thinking very slowly.

"Wondering whether maybe Ethan was too."

I cannot get my mind around what she is saying, and the fact that the static is coming more and more heavily doesn't help things at all.

Without exactly meaning to, I say: "Wait, your voice is breaking up," and I hang up, on purpose, to give myself time to think.

I know I should tell T.J. about Lucas now, about everything. But deep down, I'm afraid that if I tell T.J. about Lucas, that will mean the affair is over: I know that, like certain sinister entities, it won't be able to live in the light. And despite myself, I realize that I don't want it to be over.

When she calls back nearly an hour later, her voice is clearer, and so am I.

"Did Lucas tell Marathon that he's having an affair now?" I ask her.

"What? I don't know."

"Then what was she talking about?"

"I don't know. You're missing the point," T.J. says. "The point is not about Lucas. The point is about Ethan."

"Ethan is not having an affair," I tell her.

"How do you know that?" she asks me.

"Because Ethan hasn't had a decent erection in twenty-seven months," I say.

"With me," she says.

"At all," I say.

"No?"

"You asked me to keep track, didn't you?"

Then she proceeds to tell me a story, the kind of story that makes men gasp for air when they realize that this is how women talk. She tells me that two nights before she left for Atlanta, she came home, buzzed, from a book party, and found Ethan already asleep.

"So it's been like four *years* since I've had sex with him, right? So it's no big surprise that he's asleep when I come home, but when I look closer, I see he's kicked off his covers."

"Oh, God," I say.

"Right," she says. "It's like it was saluting me."

"What'd you do?"

She says nothing.

"Did you really?" I say.

"Yes," she says. "Well, first, I got more drunk in the living room."

"And then?"

"And then I climbed on."

"You're kidding."

"I'm not kidding."

"Well," I say. "How was it?"

"As good as it can be with someone who isn't really conscious."

I laugh. "You don't really think he's having an affair, do you?" I ask her.

"I almost wish he were. It would show a little initiative."

"When are you coming home?" I ask.

"Early next week," she says. "And I told Marathon that you'd meet her about the apartment."

"What?" I say. "Why?"

"Because. I just told you, Sally," she says. "Her husband screws around on her. She needs something positive in her life."

Once, a long time ago, I asked T.J. if she ever thought about leaving Ethan. She looked at me as if I was insane.

"Never?" I asked.

"Well, okay. Once. When I was editing Baryshnikov's book."

I laughed.

"But you know," she continued.

"What?"

"Marriage."

"What?"

"You know. It *is* the most important love in your life."

I looked to make sure she was serious, and amazingly, she was.

"Think about it," she said. "You don't choose your parents. You don't choose your siblings. You don't choose your children. All those kinds of love are just automatic. They're just nature. But marriage? That's a choice you make. And the permanence of it. That's what—that's what redeems the worst flaws in you."

She looked up at me.

"Oh, shut up," she said, and we both laughed.

"But what if you choose wrong?" I asked.

She shook her head.

"Too easy," she said. "Nothing's perfect. You stick."

I am working my hardest to remember this conversation when, five days later in Mom's apartment, Lucas sits on the shrink's leather couch, naked, a fat brown cigar in one beautiful hand and my manuscript in the other.

I am pretending to work on the doctor's shelves—not the books, which have long since been picked up by a local community center, but the endless knickknacks and figurines, in their gaudy, plaster profusion.

Occasionally, he sighs. I hate that. Occasionally, he laughs. I love that. But the pages turn far too slowly, a dull, harsh drumbeat for my regret.

I hear my father drumming his fingers on the desk that stood in this very room, and I can see him squinting into the dusk at sunset, trying to understand some foolish thing my mother has said. What would his life have been like if he'd had the courage to leave my mother and marry someone else? Would a ceiling have still fallen in on him?

On the shelf before me is a trio of porcelain canine musicians: doggie flutist, doggie cellist, doggie violinist. How could anyone have come to this woman's office for psychiatric treatment and seen these dogs and retained any kind of faith in her ability to treat them? At least my own Dr. Peterson had a relatively neutral office, albeit a bit of a problem with memory. ("Remind me why you're here," she used to say sometimes.)

Remind me why I'm here?

Lucas turns another page and emits another sigh.

"Ashtray!" he calls, and I put down my roll of bubble paper, and go to fetch him a dish.

He spreads the manuscript over his hairy chest and lets his cigar ash fall, lazily, and then smoothes the hair on his head with one talented hand.

"Well?" I say.

"You write like a dream," he says.

I smile.

"You do," he says. "I mean it," he says. "But Lord, you don't have a fucking idea what happiness is, do you?"

❋

After he has shown me what he thinks I should think happiness is, I ask him: "What *do* you think it is?"

"Happiness?" he asks.

"Yes. Happiness."

"A good fuck," he says. "A good painting. A good woman. A good meal. A good cigar."

"And if you had those five things, you'd be happy?"

"No. I'll change it," he says, sitting up, and warming to the topic. "I know what it is," he says. "It's a better fuck. A better painting. A better woman. A better meal. A better cigar."

"What about the best?" I ask him.

"The best doesn't make you happy," he says. He preens, intentionally, comically. "You should know that by now, from me," he says.

"You're saying that better is better than best?" I ask.

"Yes."

"I'm not sure I understand that," I say.

"I'll paint it for you sometime," he murmurs and hushes me up with his need for more.

I write all week. Another new beginning. Honed and polished and somewhat overwrought. I jot things down on napkins. I carry a notebook everywhere. It feels as if I'm making progress. In reality, my new outline has given me so much work to do—and redo—that it has safely placed me farther from finishing the book than I've been in months.

A new batch of letters arrives on Saturday. Katie writes about a ropes course she is taking and about her determination to zip-cord her way into the lake before the summer is over. She doesn't mention visiting day directly, but she does describe one bunkmate's overindulgence in the candy department and the girl's subsequent stomach woes. Katie sounds almost homesick when she writes about lying in bed that night. "Mommy," she writes, "I felt so bad for her. I wouldn't want to be sick so far from home."

There are two letters from Emily, which I open with trepidation, fearing I will find something even more heartbreaking. But the letters are unexpectedly brief, and they seem, if not bouncy, at least not pitiful. Then I read the postscript to the second letter, in which she scrawls: "Mommy! Guess what? You know the date on milk that you're supposed to sell it by? Well, the date on my chocolate milk container this morning said September 1!!! It's almost over!"

And indeed, though it doesn't seem possible, the second part of camp is already half done.

Then, the following Tuesday, I open the door to my mother's apartment and find that the entire huge bedroom wall has been painted by Lucas Ross with a mural of such staggering beauty that I literally sink to my knees before it.

His signature colors of black and blue cast a kind of darkness over the room, but the central figure, a man, stands in the midst of this world, exultant. And he is surrounded by five figures, and behind those figures, five shadows. The five figures are an artist's canvas, a woman, a bowl of fruit, a cigar, and a rumpled bed. And the shadows behind them are a more faded canvas, a less certain woman, a smaller bowl of fruit, a shorter cigar, and a less rumpled bed.

The woman in front looks like me.

Underneath the figures, in Lucas's white letters, is painted:

> Happiness = Change
> Best is good. Better is best.

The mural is witty, vibrant, grand, gorgeous, moving, and strong.

I am awed, unambiguously awed, by the gesture and by its beauty. It strikes me that this might be the most beautiful painting I've ever seen. It strikes me that he's actually serious about me. It strikes me that I am in the presence of genius. And, apart from everything else, it strikes me that my mother's West Side apartment has just increased in value by about two million dollars.

I can't tell if it is the beauty of the mural or the fact that Lucas has put me in it, but for a moment, I feel something that I'm pretty sure is ecstasy.

Best is good. Better is best.

What the hell does this mean, anyway? Maybe that happiness *isn't* a quality that can exist without a reference point. Maybe that being happier today than I was two days ago is enough to suggest that I am happy.

And am I happier today than I was two days ago? Oh, man, am I ever. I hug my knees to my chest, like a child, and think guiltily of the pleasure I'll feel when I get to thank Lucas Ross myself for the marvel he's painted on my wall.

I walk home with the most delicious feeling that I have the most extraordinary news to tell. This brilliant artist, my *lover,* may have just explained the subject I have been struggling with, perhaps my whole life. Something has just gone terribly right with the world.

Yet this is not uncomplicated. There is a sense of inevitability to my new understanding, but a sense of awkwardness as well. I want to shout the headlines, yet I'm aware of a need for decorum. It is not unlike the feeling I had when I first found out I was pregnant. My inner world has altered, but it is not, somehow, in good taste to tell.

At home, I virtually tiptoe through the rooms, unsteady, trying to absorb the old world and not be absorbed by it.

Best is good. Better is best.

I stand in the kitchen, and start with the mundane.

Like the rest of the drawers in my too-tidy house, the kitchen drawers are as organized as any kitchen drawers can be. There is no room for improvement here. Short of replacing them with brand-new custom cabinetry, short of discovering that they all have secret compartments filled with the elixir of life, they are the best kitchen drawers they could be. They do not make me happy. Not the way they did the week we moved into the apartment, and I realized how much bigger than my old kitchen drawers they were, and I lined them with paper, and I wrestled with the domestic geometry of utensils, baskets, and baking things. *That* was happiness. Making things *better*. That really was *best*.

Whereas.

Michael. His roadside humor and his summer-camp wisdom and his spousal tolerance notwithstanding, he seems, at this moment, to be a tidy, perfect, kitchen drawer of a person, everything in the right place, everything useful, tasteful, familiar, and certainly no surprises.

But could I leave him? Could I actually leave Michael? The friend of my childhood, my normal half? Leave him to these walls, this kitchen, these cereal bowls to fill?

Or am I just looking for trouble? Just dealing with the prospect of loss by scratching a sharp and needless pain into an otherwise healthy thing?

Into my mind, for a moment, comes the memory of a *New Yorker* cartoon: "You've made me very happy, Ted, but now I want to be miserable again."

And the girls? The girls, whom we will be picking up from camp at the end of this very week? How could I fit them into Mom's old apartment? For it does not occur to me, even for a moment, that I could now, or ever again, in fact, live anywhere else but where that painting is.

Months and months later, looking up the origin of Charles Schulz's "Happiness is a warm puppy" (first uttered by the character Lucy in a 1960 comic strip), I will learn that Schulz had once painted his daughter's bedroom wall with Peanuts characters, that new owners had painted over them, and that even newer owners had painstakingly stripped the wall and had the entire thing carted to a museum.

But that will be months and months later.

Tonight I am, on purpose, asleep by the time that Michael comes home.

In the morning, I remind him that I am going up to Boston to interview the head of the Laughter Institute. He smiles in his kitchen-drawer kind of way.

"The Laughter Institute," he repeats.

"Yes."

"That's, what, like a Monty Python thing? Like the Ministry of Silly Walks?"

"It's a real institute," I say, laughing.

"And obviously, it works."

I am on the shuttle, flying north, by just after ten o'clock. I am trying to read my notes. I am trying not to think about the blue and black image of a joyous man, surrounded by the ways he can envision and revise his life. Or the way I can revise mine.

I put the stack of papers on my lap. I close my eyes. I lean the side of my head against the cool plastic airplane paneling.

To me, the arms of the plane are the arms of the man, outstretched, and throttling space.

20

We should consider every day lost on which we have not
danced at least once. And we should call every truth false
which was not accompanied by at least one laugh.
—*Friedrich Nietzsche*

At first glance, laughter therapy would seem to be just another in
an impressive series of attempts by experts to take what's utterly
natural and sell it back to everyday people as though they had
never heard of it. Yet laughter, its proponents claim, can be a significant aid to health, lowering blood pressure, clearing lungs, re-
laxing muscles, releasing endorphins, lessening pain, reducing stress,
and improving the immune system.

"Laughter," according to the founder of the Boston Laughter
Institute, "is not only a reflection of momentary happiness but also
a predictor of greater happiness to come."

The Boston Laughter Institute, founded in 1997, offers lectures, books, videos, CDs, and instructors who will help communities set up what it calls Laughter Clubs.

HERE'S HOW TO START ONE IN YOUR COMMUNITY . . .

Run by Felicia Zelwig, a stout and mirthful woman in her late fifties, the institute is located in a town house in Back Bay, as unlikely a place as any for the serious study and promulgating of riotous intervention.

Zelwig paces behind her desk and, every now and then, stops to smile. "Smiling and laughing are two of the most natural things we do," she says. But oddly, her own smile seems vaguely synthetic. In fact, she cannot seem to smile at all while looking directly at me. When she smiles, she moves her face into a three-quarter profile, as if she long ago found her best angle and is posing for a never-present, ever-imagined photographer.

I ask her how it all began.

She tells me that she was a very somber child, a miserable adolescent, a moody college graduate, and that throughout her first twenty years, she suffered from a series of allergies and strep infections.

"Strep!" she suddenly declares and emits a laugh that is, truly, unlike any laugh I've ever heard before. It begins from some subterranean place and bubbles up toward the surface, growing in volume and size and—despite myself—contagion.

I can't help myself. I laugh too.

This makes her laugh more, laugh so hard that she literally clutches her side.

"Are you all right?" I ask her.

"Wonderful!" she says brightly, takes a deep breath, and continues. "I was twenty-five when I first learned to laugh. Up until then, I'd always been one of those bookish kids, and I didn't find anything funny. At that point in my life, my idea of happiness was maybe a really good piece of pie."

Then came a particularly bad strep infection that landed her in a hospital and brought her into contact with a Pakistani nurse named Shri.

Shri was apparently the student of a man who had created, in Pakistan and also India, a series of Laughter Clubs that were based on the belief that laughter can heal. And not just in the metaphorical sense but literally. Under Shri's tutelage, Zelwig learned how to laugh and, subsequently, how to lead a Laughter Therapy Group, the purpose of which is to create a new habit, a habit of happiness, as she calls it.

"If you laugh, even if you don't mean it, you get used to laughing, and then you wind up laughing more," she says, laughing.

While I am remembering the smiling Tibetan monks, she adds: "It only takes twenty-one days for the average person to form a habit. If we train them to act happy, they start being happy."

"Oh," I say.

And then she lets out another laugh, as if I have just said the most hilarious thing in the world, and I wonder if this is how Robin Williams feels when he is having a good night.

The highlight of any visit to the Boston Laughter Institute can be found on the upper floors, where at least three separate Laughter Therapy Groups are in session. Zelwig says she'll allow me to sit in on one of the sessions but only if I agree to participate, not merely watch.

"It's too disconcerting to the laughers to have an outsider who might be laughing at them," she explains, without irony.

"At least it would be laughter," I suggest.

She shakes her head, firmly, and so I reluctantly agree.

Here is what the sixteen of us in the room I enter have to do:

We have to stand in a circle and hold hands.

We have to inhale and exhale, the way we would in any exercise, yoga, or, for that matter, childbirth class.

Then the fun begins. The leader of the group, a perfectly sane-looking man in blue jeans, shouts out "Hah!" and we all shout "Hah!" back.

More cleansing breaths.

Then:

"Hee!"

"Hee!"

"Ho!"

"Ho!"

"Ha Ha Hee Hee Ho Ho!"

"Ha Ha Hee Hee Ho Ho!"

"Ha Ha Hee Hee Ho Ho!"

By the fourth or fifth iteration, I am, of course, completely convulsed. I am standing in a circle, surrounded by a pack of strangers, and we are all hysterical.

"And . . . *Stop!*" our leader announces, and needless to say, we can't.

On the way back to the airport, I find it hard to stop smiling. The whole scene at the institute strikes me as hilarious, and then, too, I remember lying on the grass at the girls' camp, a horizontal version of what those poor suckers are paying to learn to do, and I automatically want to tell Michael about it, but I realize that I am, perhaps irreversibly, too far from home.

The landscape of return is black, but bejeweled. Stars shine above the airplane; lights shine below, creating constellations of cities and towns that we pass on our way home.

Beside me, a woman drinks three tiny Scotches in quick succession, then leans back into her headrest, smiling. I envy her, for a moment, what seems like a gentle, smoky oblivion.

It is ten o'clock by the time I land, but I do not call Michael, despite my promise to do so. Instead, I tell the cabbie to take me to Eighty-sixth Street and Central Park West. I want to—I feel I have to—see Lucas Ross's idea of happiness, flying through space.

In the semidarkness of the back room, I sip a glass of T.J.'s white wine and sit cross-legged, like a supplicant, at the foot of this image of happiness.

I know that Michael will be worrying about me and that I should go home. But I, who have protected the past and nourished it, embraced it in a fourteen-year marriage preceded by a sixteen-year friendship; I, who am living mere blocks from the apartment in which I grew up; I, who am writing a book that is the fourth in a series of similar books—I, suddenly, am intoxicated by the concept of change.

I am back home by some minutes past eleven.

I try to make myself see it as somehow foreign, but at the same time I take instant solace in the familiarity of its walls, however badly they need to be painted.

In the kitchen, I can see the blank spot on the counter where Michael usually puts his cell phone at night to recharge the battery, so by this I instantly know that he has been on call tonight and that he has fallen asleep with the phone on his hip. I know this. I don't need to investigate further. I know that when I walk into the bedroom, I will find him asleep, with the postgame show on, on mute, because he will have had the baseball game on with the sound turned off while he fielded patients' worries, complaints, and questions.

So I don't go into the bedroom right away.

I put down my bag, and I take off my jacket, and I put my notes from the Laughter Institute on my butcher-block desk in the kitchen. Only then do I see, on the dining room table, that Michael has left me a vase of flowers, a glimmer of waiting beauty, like a lighthouse casting a beacon on an empty, unwatched shore.

21

The hours that make us happy make us wise.
—*John Mansfield*

When I was a child, my father and mother and I used to go to Cape Cod for three weeks every summer. There, I inhaled the smells of the beach plums and the salt spray; I watched the sand fleas jumping over skeins of tangled seaweed; I lived in a world in which any object that wasn't blue, white, green, or gray looked strangely out of place. I timed the sound of the surf to my heart. I dreamed of being loved for who I was, and known for what I did.

Every morning, while my mother was still lying in bed and drinking the cup of coffee that my father always brought her, my father and I would walk down the beach. Our destination was an enormous boulder in the water where terns and cormorants liked to perch; our goal was equally certain: it was to find the bits of beach glass that had washed up onshore the night before.

There was a clear hierarchy to these treasures. To begin with, a good piece of glass had to be totally rounded at the edges and totally opaque—*cooked,* my father called it. Then, as far as shape went, the largest pieces were best, closely followed by any fragments that clearly recalled the shape of the bottle: the neck, say, or the bottom. Next came color (in ascending order): white, green, amber, and best of all, blue. The pieces of blue beach glass were so rare that my father said he had sometimes spent whole vacations without finding a single one. Their discovery, whenever it happened, warranted an immediate and emphatic hug, and a kind of instant replay: "At first I thought it was just a piece of mussel shell, but then I realized it wasn't jagged at all . . ."

One day, when I was about nine years old, it occurred to me that my success at finding the blue beach glass had waned.

"I found a lot more last summer, didn't I, Dad?" I asked my father as we emptied our pockets back home.

He shrugged. "It varies from year to year," he said.

But I'd seen my mother give him a furtive glance, and later, when I was drying the dishes, I asked her about it. She smiled guiltily, glancing around to see if my father was near enough to hear us.

"He used to put them on the beach for you," she said.

"He what?"

"He'd walk ahead of you a little bit and drop them on the beach so you could find them."

I tried to take this in.

"That's why you found so many," she said.

I remember her smiling, triumphant, another small victory in her seemingly lifelong war against magic.

The next morning, I told my father that I didn't want to go with him. The morning after, I said the same.

On the third morning, he insisted I come, and together we walked down the beach to our rock.

"You lied to me," I said when we got there.

"Never."

"Every time you told me I'd done a good job! I didn't find them myself!"

"Sally," he said.

"What about the one I found last week?" I asked him. "Did you put that there, or did I really find it?"

"You know you found it."

"But why'd you do it?" I asked him, feeling both betrayed and embarrassed.

He looked at me, perhaps with more love than I had ever seen before.

"I wanted you to know how it felt," he said, simply.

"And now?"

"And now, my darling, you know what you're looking for."

22

> The greatest happiness you can have is knowing that
> you do not necessarily require happiness.
> —*William Saroyan*

*H*ome from the Laughter Institute, I go to sleep still expecting fear, or reality, or memories, to overcome my feelings, but I wake up unchanged, which is to say, changed.

Michael stands at the dresser, putting his comb into his back right pocket, his wallet into his back left pocket, his keys into his front right pocket. A place for everything, and everything in its proper place. Except, perhaps, his wife.

He turns, because he knows, without having to look, that I have just woken up.

"Morning," he says with a smile.

"Morning."

"Good trip?" he asks, and I nod.

"You writing up the interview today?" he asks.

"Interview?" I say stupidly.

"The Laughter Institute?" he says.

"Oh. Right. Well, at least I'll type up my notes," I say vaguely.

I urge my mind to focus on something, anything, that might show I know what is happening in his life. It's not that I am faltering in my desire to be with Lucas, just that I know I'm not ready to leap yet—or plummet, as the case may be. We are picking the girls up from camp in two days; I am not about to drop this bomb while the target and I are moving.

"How's Mrs. Kotlowitz?" I ask, in a desperate surge of memory.

"Kotlowitz?" he asks, his turn to be stupid.

"Mrs. Kotlowitz," I say proudly. "The stomach case."

"Oh. Discharged. She was fine."

Is this the marriage that waits for me when the girls are really gone? Was this the marriage I had before I had the girls in my life?

Girl, then woman, then writer, then wife, then mother. Adulteress. Muse? I am not so much a person as I am a set of nesting dolls. What if I'd stopped after writer and spared everyone this wooden identity game?

On the way to Mom's apartment, I stop on Columbus Avenue and buy not only a pack of Marlboros, which certainly suggests that a battle's been lost, but also a butane lighter, which is virtually a white flag.

Upstairs, I sit, as I did just twelve hours ago, before Lucas's masterpiece, and I pull the cellophane string from around the shiny pack of cigarettes as if I am tugging a ribbon off the gift of the past.

When the buzzer rings, it takes me a while to realize that it's the buzzer, and that the sound is coming from the ancient house phone over the kitchen sink. I had thought it had long since gone out of use, but its myriad coats of paint had clearly led me to wrong conclusions.

It is T.J.

"Coming up," she says.

"What?"

"We're coming up."

"No. Wait! *We?*"

Needless to say, she doesn't hear my "wait," and so I do the only thing I can think of, and that is to slam the bedroom door shut and madly search the rest of the apartment for signs of Lucas's presence. I have just enough time, before T.J. turns the key in the lock, to be relieved and amused to discover that Lucas has, in fact, left no sign of himself anywhere but in the bedroom.

The front door creaks open, and T.J. stands there like Hamlet's father, or Banquo's ghost, or someone mythical and frightening. At her side stands Marathon Ross.

"What are you doing?" T.J. has the nerve to ask.

"What am *I* doing?"

"You remember Marathon," T.J. says, giving me a God-you-look-totally-weird look.

"Of course," I say, greeting Marathon's shoes, which are patent-leather sandals in which I can almost see my reflection.

"I hope we're not intruding," she croons, sweetly.

"Well," I say, "I was trying to get a little work done."

I give T.J. a fuck-you-I-don't-look-weird-get-the-hell-out-of-here look, but apparently only I know what the look is meant to convey.

"Maybe you might want to offer us something to drink," T.J. says, as if she is slightly mortified by my terrible lapse in manners.

"T.J.," I say.

"I want Marathon to see the whole place," T.J. says. "Not that there's that much to see, you understand, Marathon. But I just know you're going to have some great ideas."

I hear the echo of T.J.'s words from a month or so ago: "She's got great taste . . . in everything except men." And I relax into the realization that Marathon is not here to reproach but to redecorate.

"I'd love to look around," she is saying now, hopefully. There is a definite hunger in her voice, a hunger that, despite my own waves of guilt, remorse, terror, envy, and anger, I can't help wanting to appease.

"I think I've got some lemonade," I say, and they follow me into the kitchen while I madly try to figure out how I am going to keep them out of the bedroom and, conversely, what kind of explanation I can give if Marathon sees the mural.

"Oh, this thing a Lucas Ross?" I might say. "No, it can't be! It's always been there. I mean, at least for as long as I can remember. You're sure? Well, my father must have copied it or something. He was very handy with stuff like this. He's dead, though, so we can't ask him . . ."

"Sally?"

I have paused, like a wound-down windup toy, at the door of the ancient freezer.

"Sorry," I say and grab for the ice tray and twist it, brutally, till the ice pops up and out. Then I bang the cubes into a pitcher, still feverishly trying to work out an answer.

"Lucas Ross? Right! That would be great." (Lots of laughter here.) "Imagine what we could get for this place if it had an original Lucas Ross. No, the tenant who lived here used to copy famous artists' work in her spare time. Unfortunately, she's dead now, so we can't ask her . . ."

This time, T.J. actually elbows me.

"What is wrong with you?" she says, plainly.

"Nothing," I say and neatly dump a packet of lemonade mix into the pitcher. "See if you can find some unchipped glasses," I say.

T.J. gives me a withering look and opens a cabinet door.

"Who lived here?" Marathon asks.

An art forger, I am tempted to say.

"A shrink," T.J. declares. She holds up a jelly-jar glass that features Fred Flintstone chasing Dino chasing Fred Flintstone chasing Dino. "Can't you tell?" she asks, and we all laugh. I pour out the lemonade, and we carry it into the living room, to sit like ladies at a tea party, not one of whom could well be terribly hurt by any of the others.

From her perch on the doctor's couch, T.J. can see down the hall to the closed bedroom door.

"The bedroom's through there," she says to Marathon. "And that's the only bathroom. It's got those old subway tiles, but I've heard they can be really spruced up. You can clean them with acid or something."

"You can't go in the bedroom," I say.

Both of them look taken aback by my tone, which is considerably more martial than I had planned it to be.

"Why not?" T.J. says.

"Oh, it's— I had the floor in there done."

T.J.'s eyes narrow. She doesn't believe me. But for the moment she says nothing, just crosses her legs and sips her lemonade and starts turning pages of the decorating magazines.

For the next five minutes, she merely darts occasional looks in my direction while simultaneously cooing over the Bermuda winter home of Michael Eisner or Michael Milken, or someone like that.

"I like bright colors," Marathon declares, which makes perfect sense to me, given the mass of black and blue that her husband has spilled over the wall in the next room.

"I think bright colors just open up a room," she says.

And so on, until T.J., as I'd known she would, excuses herself to use the bathroom, and I know that she has absolutely no need to use the bathroom, that she is just bent on discovering what it is I am trying to hide. And for my part, I am torn between, on the one hand, wanting to barricade the bedroom door with my body and, on the other hand, wanting to revel in the look I will see on T.J.'s face.

The look does not disappoint, nor does it take any time to appear. T.J. is so shocked by the sight of the mural, in fact, that she has forgotten her purported mission, and she returns from her supposed trip to the bathroom in about sixty seconds.

"Something wrong?" I ask, my turn to make her uncomfortable.

"Wrong?" she asks, more flustered than I think I have ever seen her.

"You came back so fast. Is the light out in the bathroom or something?"

"The bathroom?"

"The bathroom," I say—sternly this time, because we must be starting to sound like Lucy and Ethel.

"No," she says, recovering. "No. It's just—the fumes from the bedroom are so intense. What is it, polyurethane?"

Try oil paints, honey.

"Yes," I say. "Polyurethane."

"I don't hardly smell it at all," says Marathon helpfully.

"Well, *I* do," T.J. says, "and it's giving me a headache. Maybe we should do this another day."

I expect Marathon to leap up obediently, but she has slipped her patent-leather sandals off and tucked her feet up into the couch.

"It's just so lovely to get away," she says.

Neither T.J. nor I say anything.

"T.J.'s probably told you a little bit about my husband?" Marathon asks, rhetorically. "You know, being married to a genius is like trying to stand on the sun." And then, after that, I choose not to listen, because she is speaking a little too critically about the man I think I love. The man who, having put me in his painting, has made me believe, at least for a moment, that he may want to put me in his life.

At 7:30, the reservoir is pink and green with summer reflections, and I stretch out on the doctor's couch to light another cigarette, and lean back, as I once did in a chaise on the beach at Cape Cod.

T.J., who has put in a full afternoon's work and even picked up some sandwiches before returning to read me the riot act, eyes me nervously, clearly unsure about how or where to begin.

"Smoking," she says.

"Hmm," I say, exhaling noisily.

"I can't believe you're smoking," she says.

"That's too easy to start with," I say.

"What?"

"If you're going to chew me out. That's too easy. Of course I shouldn't be smoking."

"But why are you?"

"Because I want to," I say.

"And I suppose you're going to tell me that's your answer to the other thing—"

"No. Well, I mean, of course, yes, I want to."

"But?"

"But it's more than that. I think so, at least."

"You're sleeping with Lucas Ross for some reason other than that you just want to?"

"Can you please stop being so judgmental for two minutes?"

She shrugs.

"Are you really so disapproving? Or are you just jealous?" I ask her.

"That's too easy to start with," she says, which makes both of us laugh.

I take a last puff of my cigarette and stub it out in a peach-colored Fiestaware dish.

"You know I've spent this whole time thinking about, writing about, happiness—" I say.

"I promise you that Lucas Ross has nothing to do with your happiness," she says.

"What makes you so damned sure of that?"

"Because I know him well enough to know there's only one person's happiness that he's ever cared anything about. Look at Marathon, for Christ's sake. Look what he's done to her."

"She would have been that way with anyone," I say.

"He would have *made* anyone that way."

I get up to empty the ashtray, slightly unnerved by the point she is making.

"Look," I say at last. "You know me. You know my life. I always thought—or hoped—"

"You thought what?"

"I just want to be happy," I finally say.

She stares at me, hard.

"You have been," she says.

She means, of course, that I married my childhood sweetheart and have stayed married to him for fourteen years. She means that I've had two children, and that they are healthy, and that I've had a successful career, and that my husband is not a deeply dysfunctional wreck of a human being. Beyond this, I know she means that no one I knew personally got blown up in the World Trade Center, and that I wasn't born to live and die in poverty and pestilence, and that I don't have a deadly disease.

"You're telling me I have no business being unhappy?" I say, the words *double standard* forming on my lips, the arguments and evidence against T.J. lining up in my brain.

"Leave me out of this," she says.

"Let me just show it to you," I say. "I mean, you've really got to look at it."

For a while, T.J. indulges me, and we sit at the foot of the mural, and I realize it's different in different light. The blues become iridescent, and the lettering, which seems slightly streaked and gray in the daytime, glows white and emphatic at night.

"Good is better. Better is best," T.J. reads dutifully.

"You see?" I ask her.

"What is this piece titled, 'Fortune Cookie Number Seven'?"

"Bitch."

"What the fuck is it supposed to mean?"

"That happiness comes from being brave enough to push on to what's better," I say. "Good isn't good enough. It's better than nothing, but *better* is what's best."

"Uh-huh," T.J. says and seems to ponder this for a moment.

"It means you shouldn't be afraid of change," I say.

She stands up.

"Where're you going?"

"To get your cigarettes," she says.

"Smoking?"

She laughs, then leaves me alone with the painting. My painting.

When she comes back, she is not carrying cigarettes but one of the paper bags she had brought when she came to the door half an hour ago, so I think she has cookies, or coffee, or some special T.J. after-dinner touch. What she has, however, are two cans of black spray paint. I realize she is serious when she breaks a manicured nail prying off one of the caps.

"You cannot in any way be serious," I say.

"Can't I?" she asks.

"How could you just—apart from anything else—how could you want to destroy something so beautiful?"

"I don't know, Sally. Tell me," T.J. says, and she gives a test spray on the wall beside the mural, leaving a frowning black arc above her head.

I take the spray can away from her.

"All right," I say. "You've made your point."

"Sally," she says and grimly opens the second can. "This is not a present that you can keep."

"If you so much as scratch this wall, our friendship is over," I say.

Our eyes lock for a full thirty seconds. She yields first and asks, more sweetly than I could have imagined possible, "Are you saying you think you might actually be in love with him?"

She is not a scolding woman now. She is a girl on the brink of learning a secret.

"Yes," I say. "I'm saying I think I might actually be in love with him."

"And how does he feel about you?" she says after another quiet minute.

"Look," I say.

I point to the first woman in the painting, the woman who's me, and T.J. stares.

Without sarcasm or wit or any classic T.J. condescension, she turns back to me from the painting and whispers, "Oh my God. It's you."

And then, the next morning, I sit at the kitchen table at home and reach for my tape recorder, and in one hideous, pathological moment (is it possible, just possible, that I'm not quite as ecstatic as I think I am?) I knock over my coffee cup. On its way to the floor, it spews its dark khaki-colored contents onto—and into—my open PowerBook. The screen on the PowerBook freezes, like the last image in a dream that has been cut short by waking.

The hospital for PowerBooks is downtown, in the Twenties, in a large, converted loft with high ceilings and wood floors, where dozens of cat-faced technicians toil over hundreds of broken computers. In a waiting room funkily decorated with porch swings, BarcaLoungers, and old park benches, clients perch or pace nervously, waiting to hear their numbers called. Then, sitting face-to-face across the desk from a technician, they will hear the prognosis: the chance for a cure, the method of treatment, and of course, the cost.

I bring my PowerBook to the front desk, explain what happened, and am told to wait. My panic is so global that it forces me to move slowly, to breathe deeply, to do my best imitation of a woman who can function. Gingerly, I sit on a swing, and I grip the cold metal chain in my hand. I conduct a terrified mental inventory. Several years of research, drafts, revisions, notes, outlines, and pithy quotations. Digital photographs of the children. Databases of names and addresses. Files of ideas for future work. Children's first words and adorable sayings. Six years of financial records. All of this, possibly, soaked into oblivion by one turned-over latte.

An hour passes, then another half. What an amazing feeling, to think that the past has just been wiped out. What a horror, what a relief, what an outrage, what a gift.

Finally, after nearly two hours, a girl who looks at best a month older than Emily calls my number. I walk slowly toward her, but instead of sitting down with me, she motions me back, toward the worktables, where my PowerBook lies open, its screen a gray expanse and its keyboard propped up against it. Grimly, the girl rolls a second chair beside her own. She motions me to sit.

"Coffee?" she says, and it takes me a moment to realize that she is not offering me a beverage but confirming a pathology.

"Yes," I say. "And it had milk in it."

"I thought so," she says. "You can kind of smell it."

She has not one but two metal studs in her tongue. She is my only chance of salvation. She says that she will call me in a day or two, and that she will do everything she can to try to recover the frozen contents of my life.

"You," my husband declares when he comes home at seven from the hospital, "are an absolute, total mess."

He stands at the foot of the bed, where I have landed like Dorothy during the twister, watching while all the unmatched pieces of my life swirl by.

"How much of it did you not print out?" he asks.

"I don't know," I tell him. "I really don't know. A lot. There were notes. And two new chapters. The whole new introduction. Oh, God, Michael. I'm so screwed up."

He stares at me hard a minute.

"Have you eaten anything?" he asks me.

I shake my head.

"Have you called the garage for the car?" he asks me.

I shake my head.

"Have you packed any food for the road?"

I shake my head.

And the thought of seeing the girls is so awful. How the hell can I face them tomorrow? I'm not a plausible mother right now. I'm barely a plausible human; I'm a knot of fear and desire and confusion who seems bent on destroying as much of her life as she possibly can.

Michael leaves the room and returns a moment later, bearing a shot glass full of Scotch.

"Doctor's orders," he says and hands it to me, and after a moment, I slug it back.

His sweetness and concern are unacceptable offerings. I need time. I need space. I have to think.

Michael sees the fear in my eyes.

"What are you not telling me?" he asks, and so I take a deep breath.

"It's all this stuff—" I begin, and a tear drops down my cheek.

He catches it on his thumb and cups my cheek in his hand and bends down slightly to listen better, and I stop myself. I can't tell him now.

"This stuff—of the kids'," I say instead. "All of those great things they said. And all the pictures of them. And all the work. It's like I've lost absolutely everything."

Finally I cry, and his arms wrap around me and lock like the doors of a gate.

At night, still feeling my heart race, I watch Michael until he falls asleep. Then I walk softly into the girls' bathroom, where I open the small window wide, run a bath, slide silently into the scalding water, and smoke a cigarette.

23

If you can't be happy where you are, it's a cinch
you won't be happy where you ain't.
—*Charles Tremendous Jones*

*I*t is a humid, sultry morning, promising anyone's guess of sunshine, clouds, or rain, a perfect mirror for the confusion I feel.

Michael drives, and I don't mind. Even driving seems to involve too many decisions for me at this point.

So I fidget with the radio, the CD player, the toll money. I eat a second bagel from the bag we've brought for the girls, although I had sworn when we left the city that I would not have even one.

"You want a cigarette, don't you?" Michael asks.

"A what?"

"A cigarette," he says with a smile, but not a vicious one.

"How'd you know?" I ask him, wondering, immediately, if this is some kind of code.

"How could I not?" he says, which clarifies nothing.

I am silent. I need to hold myself back, but I am suddenly breathless to think that Michael may know something I didn't know he knew—even if that something has the power to unlink our lives.

I look for songs on the radio, hoping for something definitive about happiness that will top even Bobby McFerrin. The other night, on Apple's iTunes music store, I found 206 separate songs with the word *happiness* in the title, from Harold Arlen's "Happiness Is a Thing Called Joe" to the Drool Brothers' "Happiness Fair." But all I find today are high-pitched girls singing about forever.

"How long have you been doing it?" Michael says, and I turn off the music and stare at his profile so long that even he, with a place for everything and everything in its place, is forced to take his eyes from the road.

"How long do you think?" I ask him, realizing that if we are actually talking about smoking, and not adultery, he will probably want me committed soon.

"I'd say about a week," he says.

"And what gave me away?" I ask.

"The smell, of course," he says and adds: "You can't miss the smell of smoke."

I reach into the bottom of my purse for the pack of Marlboros that I'd stashed there the day before. I take one out. I push in the car lighter.

"No," Michael says.

"What?"

"No."

He says it harshly, dramatically.

"Michael—"

"No," he says again. "You are *not* going to smoke in this car."

"But—"

"No!"

The car lighter clicks off, ready, then ticks softly like a muffled clock. I put my pack of cigarettes back into my bag.

"Well," I say, allowing myself, for a moment, to act the injured party. "Well, we've come quite a long way since your mother's bathroom floor."

"I guess."

"You used to understand what I needed."

"No, I just used to forgive it," he says, and once again, I'm left wondering if he knows about Lucas after all.

The lineup at the camp gates is less frantic than it was a month ago. There is still excitement among the parents, but there is also a hint of quiet resignation.

Over the loudspeaker, an exhausted monotone voice is repeating: "Parents will go to their children's bunks. Campers will stay in their bunks. Parents will go to their children's bunks. Campers will stay in their bunks."

Emily and Katie are both in Emily's bunk, playing jacks on the one part of the floor that isn't covered with duffel bags, laundry bags, mildewed flip-flops, and backpacks.

Even from Emily, the hellos to us are briefer than the good-byes to the bunkmates. There are awkward hugs, Byzantine secret handshakes, whispers and giggles that could only be about boys, and finally, a merry chorus of the words "Enjoy your strawberries!"

"Enjoy your strawberries!" Katie shouts at the cabin, slinging her backpack onto her back.

"Enjoy your strawberries!" campers shout back.

A counselor comes up to Emily and nicely tugs on one of her braids.

"You, too, Emily," she says to her sweetly. "Enjoy your strawberries. Really. I mean it."

Emily looks at her feet, then looks up, smiling.

Michael and I carry the bags.

We are getting into the car when I ask, "So where are they?"

"What?" Katie says.

"The strawberries."

"What?" Emily asks.

" 'Enjoy your strawberries,' everyone said. So where are the strawberries?"

This completely convulses them.

So we load them, giggling obnoxiously, into the backseat, and we shake our heads at each other as the vacuum that their absence created fills, in a moment, to overflowing.

It seems a Zen master was out walking one day when he met with a fearsome tiger. Like all good Zen masters, this one had a way with animals, and he made his best effort to calm the beast by singing a soothing chant to him. The tiger was distracted for a few moments, but then, presumably giving in to his own nature, he lunged at the master and chased him. The master ended up at the edge of a high cliff overlooking a rocky sea.

With the tiger now about to pounce, the master slipped over the top of the cliff and hung by his fingertips to a strawberry vine that was growing just under the ledge.

Below him was the roiling sea. Above him was the tiger. Beside him now, however, two mice started to gnaw at the vine to which he was clinging.

The Zen riddle asks: What does the master do?

The students offer suggestions. The master drops into the sea. The master climbs back up to face the tiger. The master waits for the tiger to go away. The master sings the tiger a song. Of course all these answers are wrong.

What the master does is marshal all his strength to reach over and pick a strawberry that is growing on the vine. And then the master eats the strawberry, letting the juice run down his chin.

❊

"And then what?" I ask stupidly, as the girls tell me how they heard this story around a campfire one night, eating s'mores.

They collapse again, in hysterical giggles.

"What?" I ask, turning back to look at them from the front seat of the car.

"You're missing the point, Mom," Katie says.

"I am?"

"Mom," Emily says with a withering tone. "The tiger is time. The sea is death."

"Yeah, Mom," Katie says.

"Yeah, Mom," Emily repeats.

"Yeah, Sally," Michael joins in, maybe too gleefully. "I told you before. Didn't I? Happiness is this moment."

"The tiger is time?" I ask again. "The sea is death?" I ask.

"Yeah. Enjoy your strawberries," Emily says.

And though I am not entirely sure, at this moment, if the strawberries are the cigarettes in my handbag, or the lover in my apartment, or the daughters in the backseat, or the husband beside me, I know one thing for certain: Something between the sea and the tiger sounds like a good idea.

24

Where happiness fails, existence becomes
a mad lamentable experiment.
—*George Santayana*

*T*he stud-tongued girl from the computer repair place calls me
Tuesday morning while I'm in the shower and leaves a message
saying that my PowerBook is ready. She does not say how much
data, if any, she has been able to recover, and she does not sound
terribly peppy. I am about to call her back when the phone rings
again, and it's Jimmy.

"Cookie!" he says.

Immediately, I lie. "I'm on the other line," I say. "I'll call you
right back." And then I leave, wanting to put as much space between reality and me as possible, wanting to get to the apartment,
to Lucas, and his view of me.

✳

Lucas, as I've known he would, wants his reward. In creating the mural, he has shown insight, brilliance, talent, effort, and generosity, and for that combination of attributes he demands extravagant praise, repetitive thank-yous, a full-body massage, his sexual position of choice, and when that is over, another round of compliments.

I am in the mood to do all of this for him. Maybe he is my strawberries. Maybe I really will start again. Blank slate, just like my computer.

Despite the air-conditioning, a small bead of sweat staggers down Lucas's cheek, and he wipes it away with his hand.

I trace the line of his nose with my finger.

"Is that you, up there?" I ask.

"The man in the painting?"

"Yes. Is it you?"

"Of course."

"And the woman?"

He looks at me as if he is slightly disappointed, though whether he's disappointed by my presumption or my doubt, I can't be sure.

"What do you think?" he asks, which does nothing to clarify his feelings. I smile nonetheless, though whether to say I was only kidding or to say I know I'm the one I can't be sure.

Wineglass in hand, he looks at his own artwork appraisingly while I start to pull on my clothes.

"What are you doing?" he says.

"I'm getting dressed," I say.

"I'm not done with you yet."

"I'm glad," I say. "But I have to go downtown."

"Why?"

"I have to get my computer."

"Why?"

"Because I spilled coffee in it."

"Lord. You really don't want to write that book, do you?"

*

I sit beside the computer technician as, piece by piece, she shows me the parts of my life regathered. The past, it turns out, cannot be wiped away any more easily than the future can.

There are the images: a photograph of Emily when she was two. The scanned-in blueprint of our apartment. The photograph of the beach where Katie learned to swim. The holiday cards we've sent out every year for the last six years.

Then come the sounds, in a file of recorded alerts: Michael saying I love you; one of the girls as a baby, laughing.

This may be what's wrong with strawberries, I think. Happiness may indeed be *this moment,* but happiness is also sometimes the moment you want to remember or dream about.

"You've got a lot of stuff on here," the technician says.

"Yes," I say.

"You know, it would run a lot better if you freed up some of the memory."

Wouldn't we all, I think.

Finally, the files of my book come back. History of Happiness. HOH. Happy. Happiness Notes. Happiness Quotes.

"You're into happiness?" the technician says, her eyes never leaving the computer screen.

"I'm writing a book about it," I say.

"About happiness?" she says.

"Yes," I say.

"Didn't the Dalai Lama already write that book?"

I call my old shrink from a pay phone on the corner. It has been six years since I've sat in a therapist's office, but on my way out of the computer place it has hit me with great clarity that when you have been married for fourteen years and then you have an affair and then you think you're in love with your lover and then you think he can inspire your work and then you spill your coffee over that work (as well as over all electronic evidence of the life you've been living), it may be time to seek a little help.

"Hello. You have reached the office of Dr. Nancy Peterson. I'm probably with a patient right now, so leave your message at the beep and I'll get back to you as soon as I can."

Beep.

My heart is racing. Despite all my dreams of injury and rescue, I have never been good at calling doctors.

"Hi," I say. "This is Sally Farber. I've been thinking that it would be really great if I could come in for a thousand-mile checkup. Some stuff's been happening that, well, I don't know. I'd just like to talk about it. So please call me when you can." And I give her my number, and I hang up, and I take the subway home, thinking that maybe all I need is a couple of months back on Zoloft, or a good cry in her office, or a few revealing dreams.

On the subway, I see the now-familiar skin treatment ad with the yellow smiley face:

30 DAYS TO A HAPPIER YOU!

The photograph of the purported patient stares out at me, her teeth blindingly white, eyes sparkling despite the fact that some graffiti wizard has taken a pen and pockmarked and scarred her otherwise perfectly happy face.

The girls are due back at school in two weeks, and if I wait any longer to take them shoe shopping, they will have to wear their snow boots.

On the trip to the shoe store, we pass a Korean market on Broadway and Eighty-seventh Street. Inside is the vast hot-and-cold salad bar where, in my twenties and still single, I used to gather my dinner nightly with a pair of stainless-steel tongs. So I think about whether I was happier then, knowing I wasn't but might have been.

We walk past the store's bright pyramids of fruit, and I remember baking an apple pie for Jimmy Shannon one weekend when we had borrowed his father's farmhouse and I pretended I knew how to bake because I thought it would make me desirable.

A lone leaf falls in front of me, though it is still only August, and I remember staring up a side street with Emily's hand in mine when I was taking her to nursery school, and a wave of yellow leaves swept past our feet and rushed by us—bright, gorgeous, and dead.

Emily walks beside me now, just a head shorter than I am.

A tarot card reader. Could I believe in that kind of magic?

A madman, muttering. Could I ever become that crazy?

A skinny teenager, wired tight, bare-sleeved, in shorts and a pair of high, strapped shoes. Model? Hooker? Anorectic? Nothing quite computes. I know that we are both, technically, women, but did I ever stride down a street with anything like that certainty? And if I never did in my teens or twenties, what are the odds that I ever will now?

A couple kissing. Married, or lovers?

"Mom?" Emily says.

I'm staring.

"Sorry," I say. "I was just thinking."

It strikes me that the opposite of happiness isn't unhappiness but paralysis.

A stack of large black garbage bags, piled up like the boulders on the beach where I walked with my father. My father, who was only fifteen years older than I am now when he died.

A little girl clutching a wilted flower. Emily.

A beer truck. My father loved a good beer.

I can make a game of this, seeing how many steps it takes to go from the outer world to the inner. Today, they feel inseparable.

CVS, a pharmacy. Also the initials of a screening test in pregnancy that told me my children were fine. Do I want to have another child?

Clearly, I have a talent now: I can trace every single thing back to a certain, scared place in the map of my heart.

A full day after my SOS call, my shrink has yet to call me back. This is still August after all.

Rather than being inspired to reclaim the contents of my PowerBook (or, for that matter, my family), I have simply ground to a halt. It has never happened like this before. I have had wintry moments, when the chill of life has made me slow, or overtaken me on a walk, or silenced me at a mealtime. But this is different, deeper, colder.

The girls' camp trunks arrive and disgorge minor mountains of clothing and linens. Several pairs of sneakers are still damp with genuine lake-bottom mud. I fill a garbage bag or two with the unredeemable, the clothes and flip-flops just barely recognizable as the ones I purchased two months ago. The rest of the laundry I leave in a pile that I hope someone else will tackle.

At four o'clock, making sure the girls can't overhear me, I recheck the messages and dial Dr. Peterson's number again.

"Hi, this is Sally Farber again," I say. "Remember that thousand-mile checkup I was asking about? I think maybe you should think of it more as a serious repair. I really need to talk to you. Please call me as soon as you can."

On Thursday, I feign a backache, and I stay in bed all day, watching movies and taking naps. In the evening Michael climbs into bed beside me and hands me a shot glass filled with Scotch. I look at him warily, questioning.

"Drink up," he says.

I sip.

"No. Drink."

I slug it back.

"Good girl," he says. "Now tell me, exactly, word for word, exactly the message you left for her."

I tell him.

"Call her again," he says.

"No way. I've called her twice already."

"You are not trying to get a date for the prom," Michael says. "Call her again. And repeat after me. *I need to speak with you today.*"

"Really?" I say.

"Foolproof," he says. "No doctor can ignore that."

She calls me at nine that evening.

"I'm having a really hard time," I say.

"I gathered that from your message. Why don't you tell me a little about it?"

But before I can start, she asks me to remind her of a few things.

Remind me when I saw you last.

Remind me how old your daughters are now.

Remind me how long you've been married.

Then she asks: "Can you give me a general sense of what's been going on?"

A most understandable question. Yet into my mind leap a dozen different images. Lucas calling out for God. Emily weeping on visiting day. The slow-motion spill of my coffee and the piece-by-piece rebuilding of my life.

I bring the phone into the bathroom, so I'll be certain that Michael won't hear.

"Well," I say quietly. "I've been having a really hard time writing my book, and the girls went to sleepaway camp for the first time, and I started smoking again, and I've been cleaning out my parents' old apartment, and I've been having an affair with Lucas Ross, and my work got better, but just for a minute, and now I think maybe I want to leave Michael because he doesn't make me feel the way Lucas does."

There is a pause. (Remind me who Michael is?)

"Well, perhaps all that might warrant a visit," Dr. Peterson says dryly.

"I realize it's August—" I begin.

"That's all right," she says. "I can see you tomorrow at ten."

And so the next morning, I set off on the crosstown bus to sit in a faux favorite chair in a faux living room with a faux relative expressing faux fascination in the midst of a faux dialogue about a probably faux version of a life.

But oh, it is such a relief.

"I don't think I ever actually made a conscious decision that I was going to put writing second," I say, once we've landed on the subject of my work. "I don't know when the girls and Michael started to come first."

"And do you think that that would be different with Lucas?" Dr. Peterson asks with that familiar seemingly-objective-but-not-even-remotely-objective approach.

"It already has been," I say. "Lucas takes me seriously as a writer. I don't know. It's so inspiring. Just to be with him. I mean it's like sleeping with Picasso. It makes me think I can do anything. It makes me want to do my best work."

"And have you been doing your best work?"

"Well, yes," I say. "Until I spilled coffee all over it." And we have a nice, insightful, therapeutic laugh.

But then after the laughter dies down, she asks me why I think I spilled the coffee.

She asks me what it is exactly that Michael has not been giving me by way of support.

She asks me if I ever needed Michael to be my muse or my editor before.

She asks me if I didn't before, then what do I think is different now.

And while my eyes fill with tears, my mind fills with the image of a camp bus pulling out on a lifeless June morning.

25

✳

If only we'd stop trying to be happy
we could have a pretty good time.
—Edith Wharton

Jimmy calls me Monday morning.

"You never called me back," he says.

"I'm sorry, Jimmy," I say.

"You recklessly promised to call me back, and then abandoned me to my lonely desk."

"I'm sorry, Jimmy," I say.

The girls are roaming, restless, around me, and every time I move to a different room, they follow me.

"What's going on, Sally?"

His use of my actual name unnerves me.

"Going on?" I repeat.

"When am I going to see some pages?"

"Pages?" I repeat.

"Pages. Have you written any?"

Emily and Katie are pressing their forearms against each other's, trying to see whose tan is darker.

"I've written a lot, Jimmy. But I'm just beginning to realize I think I've got to redo the outline," I say.

"Uh-huh."

"I'm thinking the chronological approach doesn't work as well for this one."

"I'm tanner," Katie is telling Emily.

"No, I'm tanner," Emily says back.

"Just tell me this," Jimmy says. "Should I be worrying at this point?"

Only if you actually want to publish this book, I think.

"No, of course not, Jimmy," I say. "It's going to be great."

"Mom, whose tan is darker?" Katie asks me.

After that phone call comes the inevitable one from my mother. She informs me that she has called a thrift shop recommended by Janet McGoogan and has arranged to have what's left of the doctor's things picked up the following Thursday.

"Why?" I ask.

"It's a good thrift shop," Mom says. "All the proceeds go to the AIDS research."

"I'm not going to be ready by Thursday, Mom. I'll call them when I'm ready."

That afternoon, I am standing therefore in the old apartment, taking inventory. I have packed up all the doctor's books, all the figures and figurines, the mournful Venus de Milo, the candlesticks and vases. I've thrown out the old linens and the old shoes, most of the clothes, with their smell of mothballs and brisket and perfume. If there had ever been any good jewelry, someone ripped it off long ago, and I've put the costume stuff in a carton, along with a few of the dresses and a fur coat whose viability I don't feel equipped to judge. What's left—apart from the chairs and couches and tables and filing cabinets—are the many dusty prints on the walls, the curtains on the windows, and the area rugs on the floors.

I am just starting to roll one of these up when Marathon Ross buzzes up from downstairs and says that she needs to see me. I look around the apartment the way people do in comedies before they hide their lovers in closets, or under beds, or behind shower curtains. But the mural, by definition, is immovable, and I think it would seem strange to Marathon if the bedroom door was shut again. So I do the only thing I can think of, which is to climb up on the analyst's couch and take down the huge dust-covered Nitrolian poster and hustle it into the bedroom and prop it up on two chairs and make it cover as much of the wall as possible, which isn't much. It's like trying to hide a lion with a cat. I end up closing the door anyway.

Back in the living room, I haven't time to see what the absence of the poster has revealed, and even if I could see it, I don't think I would yet understand it.

"I had to see you," Marathon declares. She stands perfectly framed by the doorway, like a model in a viewfinder.

Even as I cower and brace myself—either to lay claim to Lucas or to apologize for everything (I haven't decided which yet)—I am struck, once again, by her loveliness, and I can't help wondering why Lucas would ever consider trading this object of beauty for something—for someone—like me.

"Oh, wow," I say, which under the circumstances, is a brilliant rejoinder on my part.

"I hope it's all right."

"What's on your mind?" I ask her, because that seems somehow neutral.

"I wanted to make some plans," she says, a slight gleam in her eye, and I think, My God, she's cool. They must learn this coolness in the South, along with this method of graceful torture.

I lead her into the kitchen.

"Plans," I repeat.

"I thought I could take some measurements," she says. "And that maybe, without T.J. here, you could tell me if this is what you really want. I wasn't exactly sure."

"Lemonade?" I ask her.

"Wine?" she asks me.

"I'm afraid I'm out," I say, surveying the contents of the fridge.

"Oh!" Marathon gasps, looking over my shoulder.

"What?"

"Oh!" she says again. "Oh my!"

She is staring into the refrigerator, at the box of Lucas's Glueck-tortes.

Why the hell couldn't I have put a poster over them?

"May I—look?" she asks politely.

She reaches two delicate hands in, as if she is extracting the mechanism of a working bomb, and holds the box appraisingly.

"These are Lucas's favorites," she says.

And before I can begin to explain or defend or lie, she says, "Would you mind if I brought one to him? He just *adores* them!"

And in an instant—maybe an instant no longer than the one in which Uncle Lysander hit the floor three months ago and Lucas's eyes hit mine—I find that I am incalculably repelled by the thought of him.

I keep Marathon in the kitchen. She drinks a glass of lemonade. Then I tell her I'm sorry, but I've decided that I'm going to rent the place out as it is, and I give her the whole box of Gluecktortes, and I send her on her way.

I leave just minutes after Marathon does and walk down to River-side Drive. The threat of being caught suddenly seems silly compared to the reality I have just witnessed: the clearly, instinctively, guilelessly generous act of a woman who clearly, instinctively, guilelessly, is in love with the man she has married.

I think back to the night in the restaurant when Lucas proposed to her, and I decide that the flush I saw in her cheeks then may not have been embarrassment after all, but something more like glee.

How can Lucas be so stupid, or so blinded by his good fortune?

Better isn't necessarily best. Better may just be whatever is different, whatever is newer, next. And perhaps all I'd wanted—fainthearted, frightened of time—was the chance to believe I could start again.

It touches me in some deep, sad way that it has taken the sight of my lover's wife reaching eagerly for a box of chocolates to make me understand this. The chocolates, I realize grimly, that are probably the only thing Lucas has ever loved with complete fidelity. Aside, of course, from himself.

"I've been thinking about it," Michael says that night, "and I've realized that you're right."

"I'm right?"

He takes my face in his hands, a gesture of unrelenting goodness. Face-to-face.

"If you want to have another baby," he says, "I think we should."

His words seem to take an especially long time to travel from his side of the marriage to mine.

"Why are you saying this?" I ask him. "And where have you been?"

He takes off his jacket, and I can see that his shirt is clinging to his back.

"Are you okay?" I ask him.

He removes the usual objects from his pockets—comb, keys, pager, phone, address book, wallet, change—and wearily returns them to their usual places.

I arrange the blankets, and my thoughts.

"I watched a patient die tonight," he says quietly when he turns back. "It was—I don't know—"

"You've watched patients die before."

"I know."

"What happened?"

"He died holding his daughter's hand. I can't explain it. Clutching her. When she finally stood up, I could see one of his fingernails had cut her hand."

Michael balls up his shirt and absentmindedly shoots it into the dry-cleaning hamper.

"Two points," I say.

"Three," he says but forgets to smile.

"Michael?"

"It isn't true what they say, you know. Some people *don't* regret not having spent more time with their families. Some people *do* regret not having spent more time at work. But this guy didn't. And I know I won't. And if another baby will make you happy, it'll make me happy too."

The world zooms back in time, a telescope closing in upon itself, and I am a thirty-one-year-old woman nursing a baby in a hospital bed. Flowers from friends bedeck the room. All I'm supposed to do is sleep and feed the baby and fall in love with her. Everything is in front of me, and nothing else matters.

Now another road is open before me, sunlit and dry and long.

Michael is waiting for an answer. I say nothing to him, at least nothing with words. I reach for him. He crawls onto me like a wave onto a shore. And moves forward and backward and forward again.

"No," I say to him after we're done.

"No what?"

"No I don't think we should have another baby," I say, and in that moment, though it seems I've taken another step away from him, I've actually taken one large step closer..

His generosity suddenly overwhelms me. Doctor. Father. Lover. Spouse. And after this, the summer of my discontent, I long shame-fully to retrieve what were once the talents of my once-generous heart. I want back our past and our future.

26

Hope is itself a species of happiness, and perhaps
the chief happiness which this world affords.
—*Dr. Johnson*

*L*ucas is outside the apartment door when I arrive the next morning.

"You're late," he says, already annoyed.

"Sorry."

"And not only that," he says. "You didn't smile when you saw me."

That makes me smile, because I believe he has just made a self-mocking comment, though later I'll start to wonder if he really meant what he said.

"We'll have to talk," I say, opening the door.

"Talk later," he says, hugging me from behind. Then we both stop and see the living room wall.

"What happened to the poster?" he says immediately.

"I had to use it," I say.

"Use it?"

"Yes."

"Use it for what?"

"To cover up your work," I say.

His brow furrows, and he darts into the bedroom. Meanwhile, I stand at the wall where, for the first time, I see a number of recessed shelves. This is no fancy arrangement. This is a vestige of West Side, prewar, nonchic: a slightly uneven hiding place seemingly chipped out of the wall plaster. Hidden by my parents' poster. Clearly undisturbed by the doctor. And revealed by me only when I'd tried to hide the evidence of Lucas Ross's presence. Perched on the dusty shelves are several objects that I strain to identify.

"I realize visual relations are not your thing," Lucas calls from the bedroom. "But you must have understood that even a five-foot-high poster was not going to cover an entire wall."

"I was desperate," I say, following Lucas's voice into the bedroom, where he has removed the poster.

"Desperate?"

"Your wife was here," I tell him and wait to see him unravel.

"Ah," he says after only a beat. "I guess that explains the Gluecktortes."

He walks toward the bedroom. I follow him.

"Oh, please," I say. "You're going to pretend that you're not curious?"

"Curious?"

"About whether Marathon saw the painting? About whether she knows what we've been doing? About why she was here in the first place?"

"*Did* she see it?" he asks casually.

"No."

"Well, I assume she wouldn't have been here unless she *did* know about us?"

So I tell him about T.J.'s misbegotten plan: to save Marathon from the too-wifely life by letting her leave her mark on this place.

"But you left your mark instead," I say, and there is everything in my heart as I say it: wonder, anger, sadness, regret.

He gives me a long and rueful look.

"I'll miss you," he says and thus denies me the chance to tell him the ending he already knows I've reached.

Calmly, he leaves the bedroom and walks toward the kitchen. My first thought is that he is planning to see if Marathon has left any more chocolates behind, but instead he bends down matter-of-factly and removes a can of paint and a roller and pan from below the kitchen sink.

"I can't keep seeing you," I tell him, which is utterly needless.

I follow him back to the bedroom, expecting something: if not a protest then at least a lovely lie or two—how with me he'd felt something different, but he knew himself too well to think he could ever leave Marathon.

But Lucas has done all the talking he wants to. And before my mind is able to understand what my eyes take in, he pops the top off the paint can, fills the tray with black paint, dips in the roller, and, starting in the lower left corner, methodically begins to paint over his own priceless art.

"Lucas!" I shout, but he keeps on going, as passionate in his destructiveness as he's been in his creativity. He paints quickly, from the outside in, in ever-diminishing borders, until all that is left of the painting are the words *happiness* and *change*. Then he wipes those out too.

"How could you just destroy that?" I ask him.

"I can always paint another," he says.

✳

It will take several more coats before the paint obscures the image of a man exulting in his choices. For a long time, the ghost of his image will remain, too vivid to be completely forgotten, but too distant to be clear.

Probably it would be lovely to care so little, to take so much, to build and destroy with such abandon, and to start things over and over again. On the other hand, it is hard to imagine a less natural existence or, in the end, a more lonely one.

So I tell him good-bye, and I give him his pack of cigarettes, and I turn back to the apartment, and the door closes behind him with a quiet click.

And what I find, in the first place, is the shelves on the wall. Perched on those shelves are dusty bottles—Mason jars, actually— and they're so dusty that it takes me a moment to see the treasures I've found.

These are my father's treasures, which were, like so much else perhaps, shining there all along. Hidden from my mother's pragmatism, hidden from the doctor's indifference. My father's jars of blue beach glass, glittering through the dust, the residue of time.

So let us say, just for the sake of argument, that happiness is the sapphire-colored glass you find on a beach you have walked many times, a beach you have known since childhood.

Let us say you need eyes keen enough to know it when you see it, and the hope and the discipline to go for the walk.

If you are not completely foolish (or a child who doesn't know better), you will not toss the blue glass back into the sea. Instead, you will put it safely in your pocket and take it home and put it carefully in a jar. And the next day you will set out again, and the next, and the next. Because a beach that has yielded such treasures before is likely to yield them again.

And if you are not completely selfish (or too blinded by your own good fortune), you will keep the jar forever, so you can love and share its contents, and so you'll have reason to keep on glancing down the long, familiar, glittering shore, to see something catch the light.

So I walk home, passing the Gap window displays, where I will watch the seasons change, and passing the pigeon footprints and the birds circling over the park, and then I sit back down in my kitchen, in the middle of my apartment, in the middle of my book, in the middle of my life—right where I belong.

Notes

Some of Sally's research into happiness is entirely fictional, and some of it is based on fact. To any readers interested in pursuing the subject, I offer the following notes as a starting point.

p. 9 *Trying to quantify happiness.* The Pleasure and Well-being Inventory (PWI) was a questionnaire given out in 1973 among citizens of Heidelberg, Germany; its respondents, revisited in 1994, showed a remarkable correlation between original levels of reported happiness and later health: the happier they were in 1973, the healthier they were in 1994. Thomas R. Blakeslee and Ronald Grossarth-Maticek, "Feelings of Pleasure and Well-being as Predictors of Health Status Twenty-one Years Later," www.attitudefactor.com/PWItecharticle.htm. The Satisfaction with Life Scale (SWLS) was developed by Ed Diener and others at the University of Illinois at Urbana-Champaign.

p. 37 *Repetitive tasks*. Annie Modesitt, *Confessions of a Knitting Heretic* (ModeKnit Press, 2004).

p. 40 *Emotional set point*. While Dr. Ellis is fictional, the set-point theory of happiness is not. It has been a focal topic of research for, among others, Ed Diener at the University of Illinois at Urbana-Champaign, David Myers at Hope College in Holland, Michigan, and David Lykken and Auke Tellegen at the University of Minnesota. See, for example, David G. Myers and Ed Diener, "Who Is Happy?" *Psychological Science* 6, no. 1 (January 1995) 10–19; Daniel Goldman, "Forget Money; Nothing Can Buy Happiness, Some Researchers Say," *The New York Times*, July 16, 1996 C1; Michael Riley, "Is Anybody Really Happy—Or Are We All Just Faking It?" Gannett News Service, February 16, 1998.

p. 42 *Happy rats*. Research into whether rats laugh—which in reality has absolutely nothing to do with the set-point theory—was being done in 1998 by Jaak Panksepp and Jeffrey Burgdorf at Bowling Green State University in Ohio. To understand the real content of their research, see "Rats Like a Laugh," BBC News, May 1, 1998, news.bbc.co.uk/1/hi/sci/tech/85711.stm.

p. 46 *Married Americans have reported themselves to be happier*. Karlyn Bowman, "Living Happily Ever After: Marriage Under the Microscope," citing a National Opinion Research Center—General Social Survey, online at www.ropercenter.uconn.edu/pubper/pdf/pp103c.html.

p. 46 *Think twice about living in Northern Ireland*. Ibid., citing Steven Sack and J. Ross Eshleman, "Marital Status and Happiness: A 17-Nation Study," *Journal of Marriage and Family*, vol. 60, no. 2, May 1998, 527–536.

p. 46 *Fewer psychiatric and medical problems*. Ibid., citing Robert H. Coombs, "Marital Status and Personal Well-being: A Literature Review," *Family Relations*, vol. 40, no. 1, January 1991, 97–102.

p. 46 *Only the happier people.* R. Lucas, A. Clark, Y. Georgellis, and E. Diener, "Reexamining Adaptation and the Set Point Model of Happiness: Reactions to Changes in Marital Status," *Journal of Personality and Social Psychology* 84, no. 3 (March 2003), 527–539.

p. 46 *Rutgers University think tank on marriage.* "Researchers: Marriage Doesn't Make You Happy; Study Found Outlook on Life Mostly Same Before, After Tying Knot." March 17, 2003, www.cnn.com/2003/HEALTH/03/17/marriage.poll.reut/index.html.

p. 58 *Hidden benefits of nicotine.* "Nicotine Releases Chemicals in the Brain/The Addiction Process," www.texmed.org/cme/phn/ndt/process.asp.

p. 66 *Tibetan monks.* Mirzakarim Norbekov, a Russian researcher, studied Tibetan monks and the healing effects of smiles within their monastery, where the rule is that everyone wear a smile at all times. Marie Snider, "Smile—A Prescription for Health, Happiness," *Fort Frances Times & Rainy Lake Herald,* July 30, 2003, www.fftimes.com.

p. 94 *Prescription for happiness.* Martin Gumpert, *The Anatomy of Happiness* (New York: McGraw-Hill, 1951), 4–5.

p. 95 *The achievement index.* Krishna Mazumdar, "Measuring the Well-beings of the Developing Countries: Achievement and Improvement Indices," *Social Indicators Research* 47, no. 1 (May 1999), 1–60.

p. 129 *What people think will make them happy.* Jon Gertner, "The Futile Pursuit of Happiness," *The New York Times Magazine,* September 7, 2003, 44.

p. 145 *Advertising.* See Richard Stivers, *The Culture of Cynicism: American Morality in Decline* (Cambridge, Mass.: Blackwell Press, 1994), 15.

p. 145 *Mansion of Happiness.* Directions for playing at www.hasbro.com/pl/page.game_and_toy_instructions/letter.M/dn/default.cfm.

p. 145 *Be Happy game.* www.1heart.com/happygame.html.

p. 145 *Harvey R. Ball.* "Harvey R. Ball, Inventor of Smiley Face,

Dies at Seventy-nine," Associated Press, April 14, 2001, and www
.smileycollector.com.

p. 153 *Epicurus.* Brad Inwood and L. P. Gerson, eds., *The Epicurus Reader: Selected Writings and Testimonia* (Indianapolis: Hackett,
1994).

p. 155 *Beyond Therapy.* President's Council on Bioethics, *Beyond
Therapy: Biotechnology and the Pursuit of Happiness* (Washington,
October 2003). See chapter 5, "Happy Souls." Online: www.bioethics
.gov/reports/beyondtherapy/chapter5.html.

p. 156 *George Mason.* For example, see Pauline Maier, *American Scripture: Making the Declaration of Independence* (New York:
Knopf, 1998), 165.

p. 156 *Robert Darnton.* Robert Darnton, *George Washington's
False Teeth: An Unconventional Guide to the Eighteenth Century*
(New York: Norton, 2003), 98.

p. 166 *Groningen Enjoyment Questionnaire.* "The Groningen Enjoyment Questionnaire: A Measure of Enjoyment in Leisure-Time
Physical Activity," *Perceptual Motor Skills* 90, no. 2 (April 2002),
601–604.

p. 168 *PBS sponsored a photo contest.* www.pbs.org/jefferson/
pursuit/contest.

p. 187 *Laughter Institute.* There really is a laughter therapy movement. It seems to have originated in India with a doctor named
Madan Kataria, who founded something called the Laughter Club International. Studies have appeared in journals of nursing about the
purported effects of laughter on the immune system. Although the
procedures described in this chapter are based on descriptions of vis-
its to real laughter clubs in the United States and elsewhere, Felicia
Zelwig is an entirely fictional character.

Acknowledgments

For their insights, help, and encouragement, I very much want to thank Donna Ash, Susie Bolotin, Betsy Carter, Cathy Cramer, Liz Darhansoff, Sharon DeLevie, Deborah Fields, Henry Grunwald, Gary Hoenig, Jonathan LaPook, Kate Lear, Kate Medina, Lynn Novick, Becky Okrent, Dan Okrent, Danielle Posen, and Anna Quindlen.

My daughter, Elizabeth, and my son, Jonathan, offered me wisdom and plot suggestions far beyond their years, and I will be lastingly, lovingly grateful for their patience and encouragement.

My husband, Stephen, not only had the fortitude to wait out (and read!) the first 3,000 versions of this book but the extraordinary generosity to insist I write the 3,001st.

Whatever Makes
You Happy

LISA GRUNWALD

A Reader's Guide

A Conversation with Lisa Grunwald

Question: In the beginning of the novel, Sally seems to have it all: the perfect husband, two wonderful children, and a comfortable lifestyle in New York City. But we learn quickly it isn't that simple. Do you think Sally is an everywoman, that it's impossible to really have it all? Or is she different somehow?

Lisa Grunwald: I meant, for better or worse, for Sally to be something of an everywoman, because a vast slice of American women in the twenty-first century do indeed, from any objective standpoint, have very little to complain about. Yet the search for happiness, or perhaps for a deeper experience of happiness, is something they also seem to share.

Q: Your novel is an interesting character study, both of individuals and of couples. How did you create such realistic yet different dynamics between the book's couples (Sally and Michael, T.J. and Ethan, and Marathon and Lucas)?

LG: I think that if it strikes readers that way, it may be because in one of my many earlier drafts of this novel, there was actually an equal focus on all three women, and thus all three couples.

Q: Sally's relationship with her mother is pitch-perfect. How did you construct such an overbearing yet still loveable character?

LG: This was one of those strange things that sometimes happens when you write fiction. My own mother died when I was twenty-one and was not, in any case, at all like Sally's mother. She's really not based on anyone I know, at least not in her entirety. Yet she really did seem quite real to me as well. I can't explain it any better than that.

Q: T.J. and Sally are, in a lot of ways, opposites (with different careers, home lives, and opinions of Sally's affair). What do you think their friendship adds to the story? What do the two women learn from each other?

LG: On the one hand, I think T.J. serves as a kind of reminder for Sally of the silliness that searching for happiness can involve (the happiness candles, the "relaxation system"), as well as of the transparency of using work to escape one's problems. On the other hand, it's T.J. who ultimately gives voice to a defense of marriage, and in many ways that is an even more profound lesson.

Q: Lucas's art plays a big part in his courtship of Sally. How, and why, did you decide to make him an artist? And what's the significance of his artistic style (the signature colors, the simple phrases)?

LG: I felt Lucas needed to be an artist because I wanted him to appeal to the deeper side of Sally: the restless, probing, and yes, less happy side of her. Unlike Michael, whose work is entirely practical, Lucas has a creative and obviously brilliant career, and that is obviously attractive to Sally. As far as his style goes, I knew it needed to make some use of words, in order for him to convey his message about happiness directly. And the rest—the signature colors, and so forth—was just me having fun.

Q: Katie and Emily's experiences at summer camp make for an interesting break in the action of Sally's life. Do you think the girls had to leave for the summer for Sally to go through everything she experienced? Did you make a conscious effort to give the girls decidedly different camp experiences? Why or why not?

LG: The girls' leaving for camp is absolutely the trigger for Sally's experiences. At one point I thought about calling the novel *The Summer of My Discontent* because without that pseudo–empty nest, I don't think Sally would have had the affair. It's not just that she has the time and space with the girls away. It's the fact that their absence really frightens her into a crisis about the meaning in her *own* life. As for the girls' different experiences, those are—like the characters of the girls themselves—very much intended to support the theory that some aspects of happiness are simply engendered by our natures.

Q: What do you hope readers will take away from reading *Whatever Makes You Happy*?

LG: Other than the desire to buy all my previous and future books? I hope, first of all, that they take away some solace in the notion that if they sometimes have a difficult time experiencing some of the joys in their lives, they're not alone. And second, even if they've reached a point where it seems that they're on the wrong path, that they know the next piece of blue beach glass may be glittering just up ahead.

Q: In your acknowledgements, you thank your own children for their wisdom and plot suggestions. How were they able to add to the story?

LG: My son, who was eight at the time, came up with the idea of hiding the blue glass behind a poster. Until then, I was stumped about how Sally was going to find it. And my daughter, who was twelve, gave me endless wisdom during a series of beach walks we shared, where she managed to ask just the right questions. Having said that, I'd add that neither of them has read the book, and neither is too thrilled with the thought that someone might think there are autobiographical elements in it!

Q: You've written works of fiction, nonfiction, and a book for children. Which genre do you most enjoy? Which is the hardest to write? The easiest?

LG: I'd rather write a sentence I love than do just about anything else, and it doesn't much matter in what genre that sentence appears. In a larger sense, though, fiction is for me both the hardest and ultimately the most rewarding.

Q: What are you working on now?

LG: I'm writing a new novel, this one based largely in the 1940s and '50s.

Questions and Topics for Discussion

1. At one point in the novel, Michael tells Sally that happiness is "this moment." What is T.J.'s definition of happiness? What is Lucas's definition? Do you have a personal definition of happiness?

2. Grunwald uses beach glass as a metaphor to describe Sally's own definition of happiness. What is the difference between Sally's beach glass and Michael's "this moment"?

3. What is this book trying to say about happiness?

4. What, if anything, does Sally gain from her affair with Lucas? Why does she pursue him—or allow herself to be pursued—in the first place?

5. One of the quotes in the book is from Victor Hugo, who said, "The greatest happiness of life is the conviction that we are loved." Does this maxim hold true in the novel? Do you believe that being loved is a requirement for happiness?

6. What is the importance of the death of Sally's father to the rest of the story? What is the connection between loss and happiness, in the book and in life?

7. Sally's two children are very different from one another, in terms of how outwardly happy they seem. Are some people born happy and others born unhappy? Do you think there is a a basic level of happiness or unhappiness to which individuals naturally gravitate?

8. Do you think that the book has a happy ending?

9. Do you think of happiness as a luxury? Do you think of it as a right? Is our culture too obsessed with the idea of happiness?

10. When you hear the word "happiness," what is the first thing that comes to mind?

LISA GRUNWALD is the author of the novels *New Year's Eve, The Theory of Everything,* and *Summer.* Along with her husband, Stephen Adler, she edited the anthologies *Letters of the Century* and *Women's Letters.* Grunwald is a former conributing editor of *Life* and a former features editor of *Esquire.* She and her husband live in New York City with their son and daughter.

ABOUT THE TYPE

This book was set in Sabon, a typeface designed by the well-known German typographer Jan Tschichold (1902–74). Sabon's design is based upon the original letter forms of Claude Garamond and was created specifically to be used for three sources: foundry type for hand composition, Linotype, and Monotype. Tschichold named his typeface for the famous Frankfurt typefounder Jacques Sabon, who died in 1580.